NEVER WAS

Sam!
Great to meet you!
H.

NEVER WAS

A Novel Without A World

H. Gareth Gavin

Cipher press

Published in the UK in 2023 by Cipher Press

105 Ink Court
419 Wick Lane
London, E3 2PX

Paperback ISBN: 978-1-7397849-6-6

eBook ISBN: 978-1-7397849-7-3

Copyright © H. Gareth Gavin 2023

The right of H. Gareth Gavin to be identified as the author of this work has been asserted by him in accordance with the Copyright, Designs, and Patents Act 1988.

This book is in copyright. Subject to statutory exception and to provisions of relevant collective licensing agreements, no reproduction of any part may take place without the written permission of the publisher.

This book is sold subject to the condition that it shall not, by way of trade or otherwise, be lent, re-sold, hired out, or otherwise circulated without the publisher's prior consent in any form of binding or cover other than that which it is published and without a similar condition including this condition being imposed on the subsequent purchaser.

Image credits
p78 Courtesy of West Chesire Museums, Lion Salt Works
p204 Courtesy of Weaver Hall Museum & Workhouse
p271 Courtesy of Cheshire Archives & Local Studies

Printed and bound in the UK by TJ Books Limited

Distributed by Turnaround Publisher Services

Cover Design by Wolf

Typeset by Laura Jones

www.cipherpress.co.uk

Apology
1

Navigation
3

—

A New Beginning
5

An Old Story
55

—

Exegesis; or, Finasteride
305

Miss Universe's Last Word
317

Apology

In lieu of a constant recognisable world, what follows might be imagined as taking place at the precise point whereupon a lightbulb, balanced on the nose of some young handsome body, turns out in fact to be a sun, done with the day, collapsing. I am sorry I could not say this more simply. I am not sorry I have said it so simply. The weather in *Never Was* whistles so many forgettable melodies that the true form of each becomes unintelligible, and you, so desperate to remember yourself, try to stay the avalanche with explosives, and you do it too soon, and you do it much too late, and then one day you wake up to the realisation – it fell upon you centuries ago, you just could not know how to come to it – that the snow is no longer a horrible obstacle, that what you have lost is not lost on you, and that your true form – yours too – has the hard contours of everything your body has ever wanted. Even while you were collapsing, you were there, tentatively balanced on your own cold nostrils. All that could have been otherwise – that too will come to have been nothing.

Have you ever wondered whether fame just accelerates what was, already, wrecked about somebody? That it is not that fame astonishes a body to the point of impossibility and sabotage, but instead some prior wreckage that, via fame, flourishes? It's also possible to imagine what follows as a way of wondering about this question, or at least, a similar one. The weather in *Never Was* is as unpredictable as it is consistent; the weather in *Never Was* is without causality. It snows both constantly and never at all, just as I am forever unseasonable. I want also to say that when I say *fame*, fame may be taken in its more ancient connotation – for infamy, for what sickens in me, and for the sort of courage that some mistakenly take for vain reluctance, or wild sorrow.

Navigation

To get to the end of *Never Was*, you have to go through two phases and several hidden ones. The first – 'A New Beginning' – is akin to a fable that actually happened; it doesn't last long. The second – 'An Old Story' – has more the look of reality but by itself is unable to communicate what really went down when, once upon a time, some young body wished the world would die, and I crossed my heart, and all that was left, after all, was just the way you wore it. It's a crime story in disguise – nothing is murdered and no body is sorry.

Each phase leads on to the other, and each is the other's alternative ending. They interlope and overlap too, but though each has of the other heard – though each of the other hums – something stays between them still. They are worlds apart, and *Never Was* is not their sum total. For as everybody who goes there knows eventually, *Never Was* is neither here, nor there, nor anywhere.

A New Beginning

The party was, as by then they always were, an afterparty. Bodies clawed the tiles and crawled crablike into the garden, which lilted down from the mansion's terrace, which sank into the lilac sunrise. Beyond the garden where the beach began, actual crabs maneuvered between scraps of plastic and antique condoms, some of which had become tangled with the crabs' rear legs, and now trailed behind them like latex bridal trains. The crabs made good brides somehow, though it did not seem as if there was anything or anybody they were marrying – their maneuvers had no future; they fussed and bustled for nothing but the fun and cruelty of fussing and bustling.

Some bodies from the party, those that had been able to crawl far enough, watched the crabs. Then they stopped and watched the sea instead. The waves heaped heavily. The foam that gushed from them was thick and glutinous, melting with jellyfish, and everywhere decorated with polymer ornaments – bottle caps and bottle cap grips, weed-kissed Tupperware, vibrantly-coloured shampoo microbeads. The bodies watching could not see the microbeads, but they could taste them – for the sea air, by then, was made of them.

Between the beach and the mansion's garden there was no real boundary, only dunes, and then between the dunes and the garden, something called a 'Ha Ha', a ditch whose descent into the earth was extremely severe on one side, soft and gentle on the other. It was there, a little apart from the party and the bodies that crawled from it, that Fin stood, on the edge of the Ha Ha's severe side, facing seawards, toes touching the turf where the turf began to relinquish itself, thinking of how the world must have been when the world had still had seasons – or had seemed to.

Two faint moons faded slowly from Fin's eyes, which were lilac like the sunrise, which already was glittered with snowfall.

Or were what seemed in Fin's eyes to be moons two bodies, not celestial? Fin squinted, and saw one body bent on all fours, the rope around its neck gripped by a second, erect body.

Then Fin squinted again, and saw a walker, and attached to the walker, a dog. The walker waited patiently while the dog shat, then carefully collected the shit in a dainty green bag, then carelessly tossed the bag to the dunes. The dog moaned. The walker looked about and caught sight of Fin, whose eyes were still on the walker, who now scrambled after the bag that had landed halfway up the bank of the nearest dune. Fin laughed. The walker was a fool, Fin thought, a fool for whom actions had consequences – the sort of fool who still believed in the world, therefore. Tickled by this thought, Fin again laughed.

Laughing hurt. Fin thought about going back inside and finding something soothing to drink, a Pepsi maybe, but couldn't face it.

For the time being, at least, Fin couldn't face having to be Fin.

For you see, Fin had been famous ever since Fin could remember. That was really the only thing worth knowing about Fin – it was the only thing *Fin* knew about Fin, it almost seemed. Fin's fame fell over everything, was everywhere and inescapable. The pain in Fin's throat was fame, the recklessness and impetuousness, the endless apocalyptic parties just like this one – those were the fame too. It had come to the point where Fin could not recall what life had been like before fame and nor did Fin have any idea whether fame had changed everything or whether Fin was just exactly the same as always – famous, somebody who belonged to everybody else, a murder case without a murder. A murderer?

In a lazy attempt to ease a deep agony in the throat, Fin gulped. It hurt to gulp – it hurt so much that it seemed Fin's voice might finally be lost, gone with the world. For that was the only other thing worth knowing about Fin, or so Fin for one felt, stood there watching the bodies of the dog and walker deplete as they scrapped across the sand dunes – Fin was somebody who no longer believed in the world.

Still, the party was a good party. Fin was just enough broken by it to feel at ease at last, in sync with the brittle reek of the sea and untroubled by Fin's troubles, which even though they still washed upon Fin's thoughts, seemed now placid and weightless, the opposite of the waves that welted the shore, watched not by Fin but by those other bodies. Fin sniffed. The sea air smelt not unlike mephedrone cut with ketamine. Or else Fin had just consumed such a quantity of those chemicals – each dose neatly cut to a slither, each slither snorted via a straw finely striped with fluorescent orange – that every smell, forever, was stained by them. Fin blinked into a tumble of snowflakes. The snowflakes seemed like metaphors for nothing, or like metaphors for something that the world – or what would have been a world, had Fin still believed in it – no longer, itself, remembered.

The way the snow was cresting the dunes made the dunes look, Fin thought, like small mountains. The snow accentuated the sand's creases, the way the sand had of lapping itself like skin that had lost its collagen. Fin touched Fin's face anxiously, feeling for wrinkles.

Once upon a time, when wrinkles were for Fin no more than a fiction, something that wouldn't happen really, and before the world became unbelievable, Fin had been to Miami. Fin had not been there long enough to be able to say that Fin had lived there. Nor had Fin seen much more of Miami than Fin had seen of other cities. But Fin had been there, definitely, because it was there that Fin remembered falling fast asleep in the arms of somebody who once had been Miss Universe. Fin had found this fact wonderful. What did it *feel* like, Fin had asked, in the fake gloaming of the changing room; Fin was particular about the lighting in changing rooms, and often dimmed the lights personally. It felt spectacular, Miss Universe had answered. It felt – it felt like being Miss Universe. That sounds *so* perfect, Fin had whispered, head at rest in the fragrant dimple of Miss Universe's inner elbow. What colour was your costume?

Miss Universe had not been able to say, however, so after a while Fin had suggested turquoise. No, it couldn't have been turquoise, Miss Universe had answered, frowning, almost, Fin had thought, horrified – for then when we stood with our backs to the sea to be photographed, my costume would have clashed with the water. It would have destroyed the composition, the difference between background and foreground.

Fin had left Miami the next morning.

The pilot of the jet by which Fin left told Fin that Miss Universe was not who she said she was, but that that was why she had won Miss Universe, and also that a storm was coming; Miami was going under. Fin had stared at the shrinking beach beneath, no longer knowing what to believe, thinking about the feeling of feeling like being Miss Universe.

Wondering why Fin should be thinking, now, at this moment, of Miami and Miss Universe, Fin blinked into another tumble of snowflakes. Fin's left foot was hovering nonchalantly above the brink of the Ha Ha, which could not be seen from the windows of the mansion, which Fin was facing away from. From somewhere off beyond the dunes came the sound of a dog barking. At first Fin didn't think to attach the bark to the dog that had passed by a moment ago. The bark just hovered in the brittle air not unlike Fin's foot above the Ha Ha. But even when Fin did remember the dog, Fin wasn't convinced the bark belonged to it. For there was nothing in the world to say that the dog and the bark were joined, irrevocably, and what was more, when the thought of the dog and the bark as one was gone, tossed away, Fin could enjoy the feeling of everything being fleeting – and inconsequential.

Although it was not actually all that cold, and not because Fin wore but a T-shirt, Fin shivered. The thought of all the things Fin had done had just now tumbled from Fin's memory, landing in full view in front of Fin not unlike a little bag of dogshit.

Or had all those things been done to Fin? Was Fin guilty, or not guilty?

Before Fin's eyes a snowflake frittered, forgetting its way to the ground. Fin watched it, wondering whether or not it frittered in sympathy. Fin thought so, probably. Probably not, actually. It didn't really matter. Then Fin sighed, and thought about the world again.

The idea of the seasons had survived far longer than had the seasons. The world had been sustained by them – by the thought of the autumn and the spring, the summer and the winter, and by the feeling of transition and rhythm that calling the months by those familiar names continued, for some time, to provide. For some time it had not seemed to matter, much, that the summer months were often and oftener swamped by rains in places where hardly any rain had come previously, or that winter was cool but not vicious, still T-shirt-friendly, or that ice cream parlours were flourishing by late February in parts of the world that once for the first months of the year had been nothing but slush and the sorry gurgle of road gritters. Everybody who was anybody still said the word *summer*. Those that preferred the cold to the hot still hankered, in their hearts, for *winter*.

Just a few moments ago – it could as easily have been hours – Fin had been sat on a settee in the mansion's living-room telling a fellow broken body of how, when on tour and travelling between stadiums nightly, it had seemed to Fin that it was Fin who was wrong, off, all over the place. There was never very much daylight. There was always a coach with frosted windows or a plane or a helicopter. Fin's fingers twizzled in bad mimicry of a helicopter's rotary wings when Fin said the word *helicopter*. It was never the same weather for more than a day, or what Fin took for a day, but Fin had still come to the conclusion that it was Fin who was the problem, who had the problem, which was the problem. What was wrong, was *Fin*, Fin had thought – and not the world, and not the weather.

It probably had not helped that by then Fin was already heavily laced with whatever chemicals Fin could get hold of – uppers of any sort for breakfast, a meal often eaten when the sun was collapsing under the first boom of stadium floodlights; opiates at first because of the strain in Fin's knees, later out of sheer habit; ketamine at bedtime because the bounce of it helped Fin sleep better; a constant popping of ibuprofen; acid, obviously; never, for no good reason, except possibly because of the calories, alcohol.

The body on the settee sat next to Fin had flinched at that, then stopped sipping a beer and set it down on the glass-topped coffee table, which Fin's torso was again folded over, dosing more lines and cutting them. By then the living-room was no longer as thick with bodies as it had been. In one of the corners stood, absurdly, a hefty stone sundial. In the corner opposite was a grand piano, white, its hood littered with silver photograph frames, some containing photographs of Fin, one a signed photograph of Miss Universe, others nothing. Fin had clocked the other body looking at the frames and grinned, obnoxiously. Fin had been about to explain why some of the frames were empty when suddenly another body was to be seen crawling beneath the coffee table, rolling over, and licking the underside of the glass. The effect was disgusting. The mark the lick left was like a sweat patch.

Fin frowned at the body beneath the glass, the cause of the disgusting effect. Then a grin obliterated Fin's frown. Then Fin continued.

One morning or one night or whenever it was, and as to where, anywhere, it had come to Fin that it wasn't Fin who was wrong. No, it was the *world* that was wrong. But even then – even then, said Fin, having come up for breath from the coffee table and, it seemed, for emphasis, because this bit was important – it wasn't that the world was wrong because the world was ruined or whatever, because actually, in reality – this is what Fin had said then, having bent back down and snorted – the world was wrong because the world, itself, was ruinous. The world wasn't ruined. The world was *ruinous*. The world was wrong because there was no world except the wreckage the world itself wreaked. There perhaps had never ever been anything except the wreckage of the world, said Fin. The seasons had forever been a cruel dream and what for some seemed ordinary, such as the drinking of tea, was in truth catastrophe. Even the end of the world was a mirage, said Fin, a children's book – a cliché.

Fin lost the other body at that point.

I know, because that body belonged to me.

I never asked, when I could have done, what it was that had changed Fin's viewpoint – I never asked what had given Fin to understand the end of the world as but another season, a bitter whim of a world that was itself a bad joke told by nobody. A bad joke told by nobody! The thought of that saddened me. It seemed to me something must have happened to make Fin think that way, something massive, or else that Fin had done something, something terrible, and the terrible thing had changed Fin. But I never asked. I just watched Fin.

I watched Fin fiddle in a pocket for the straw via which the lines of ketamine were soon to zoom up our noses.

The sight of the straw, when finally Fin found it, made me think of children's parties in McDonald's, and Ronald McDonald's body, and the gates that separated the party area off from the main restaurant. I remembered the stories, always to me so sexual, of fingers found in hamburgers and sacs of puss erupting in Chicken McNuggets, and how much I had liked the gherkins. I almost started crying again – I had been found crying earlier in a toilet by somebody whose name I now had no memory of. Fin finished a line and offered the straw to me. I took it. Tiny clusters of powder crystalled the skin beneath Fin's nostrils. I thought about pointing this out to Fin, but didn't. Fin would either not give a fuck, I thought, or else get annoyed and stop talking to me.

It was the first time I had been to Fin's mansion and I had not been invited; nor was I used to parties in such surroundings. I had just come because somebody had heard the party was happening from somebody else, somebody who knew Fin, or was in some way close to Fin, and who had known how to get here. We had driven towards a forlorn horizon across fields and, I thought, an old airport. It was possible the airport was a different memory – that the memory was old, not the airport. When I thought about it, I wasn't even sure I remembered the drive. Had I walked here? Where *was* here? For you see, by then I was already broken.

Before I met Fin, I often thought about walking out on my life. Not in the sense of taking off with whatever money I had and keeping going until the money ran out, and not in the sense of adopting a new identity completely. I didn't want disappearing to be an activity, something I had to *do*, something to accomplish. I wanted my disappearance just to happen to me – but at the same time, stupidly, I wanted to be responsible for it. If I thought about suicide, it was only in an idle and ineffectual way. What excited me more was the thought of what might happen if I gave up on things gradually, in a way that would have been imperceptible even to me – if I started washing my hair less regularly, then never; if I stopped cutting my nails and brushing my teeth; if I stopped taking care of all the little things it was necessary to take care of to get through a day. Would I get through the day anyway?

I always did, or always seemed to. The next day came relentlessly. Deep down I knew such thoughts as these were themselves a sign of how far I was from really disappearing, or from manufacturing my disappearance so that it would seem I had *been* disappeared – so that it would seem that my disappearance had been done to me, but not by anybody but me. What stopped me? It wasn't that my life was precious to me. But I was precious about *it*, definitely.

There were a number of times when I had plummeted, but each time I'd recovered, and each recovery was horrible because each recovery was, I thought, a gross disloyalty. To what though? I wondered. It was as if I was desperate for everything to remain absolutely temporary, so that something could be as if it had never been, so that I could be untouched by it. During the periods of time when I was a smoker, I would buy tobacco but not rolling papers. I was always without my own lighter. After hating cats for most of my life, I got two, and watched them hunt flies for a week. When they gave up, having found no flies to hunt, I watched the world die in their eyes.

Even when I didn't know what Fin was talking about when Fin talked about the end of the world, or the end of the end of the world, I knew what Fin was talking about. The world was already over, Fin said, it had happened right under our noses.

That was funny.

My name, by the way, is Daniel, though nobody calls me that.

That was exactly what I said to Fin by way of introduction – that my name was Daniel, though nobody called me that.

I was already high from the line Fin had given me. I was so high I could hardly say my own name. I was fizzing and sinking and bouncy. I was somebody else's out-of-body experience and so, it made complete sense to me when, with a kink of Fin's hand through eternity, Fin announced that this, *all this*, everything that was happening right now, was in reality Fin's future memoir, and then asked me whether I wanted to be in it.

I stared again at the empty photograph frames, then looked about just in time to see Fin exiting the living-room. I felt a fan's thrill then, that feathery intimacy that seems as if it will tickle forever if kept carefully, like George Michael's invisible lip marks on a glass kept unwashed by an air steward. I couldn't have said why exactly, but I would have done anything to be in Fin's memoir. I would have killed to be. I was elated and my memory was a snowflake taken like ecstasy on the tongue of a body that was not mine. I was overtaken with a feeling of necessity, a feeling that was strange to me, and for which I felt an intense gratitude.

But at the same time I was puzzled, because it was then, when I was still sat on the settee in the living-room, the eyes of Miss Universe all over me, the stone sundial stood there so hopelessly, that I realized I wasn't actually sure that I had ever heard of Fin. All I knew was that Fin was supposed to be famous, and I had only come here because somebody had been told by somebody else, somebody in some way close to Fin, that Fin was having an afterparty.

I got up and went to the living-room's large window and pushed apart the curtains, then watched Fin sink with the slope of the terrace into the garden. The sun was just beginning to rise. From somewhere the other side of the mansion I heard the sound of an engine coming to life with difficulty. Somebody was leaving. For a moment I thought I too should leave, but the thought quickly frittered away from me, and instead I pressed my nose to the glass the better to watch Fin walk into the distance. Fin's footprints were fast obscured by snow, which fell somehow both lightly and lush upon Fin, who moved somehow both nimbly and slow – like a shadow that had never had the bother of being attached to a body.

There was, I thought then, something ancient about Fin, something at once familiar and empty, as if Fin were an aggregate of many things I had read or dreamt about but only known in bits and pieces. Or was it the scenery that I recognized – the mansion and lilting garden, the snow, the tender sunrise? But why ever would such things be familiar to me? I suddenly felt like a spare part at a party, then remembered, with a pang, that I was. I pressed my nose harder against the glass. Whatever it was that was ancient about Fin was, I thought, awful in an ancient sense too – full of awe, and frightening.

By then some bodies that had crawled to the shore had found the energy to heave themselves up again, and crawl backwards, and shovel their bums into the sand dunes. For the time being the tide was coming in, divorcing the crabs from their condoms, burying the hornwracks, which were easily mistaken for seaweed but which really were tiny bryozoans, or moss animals. The sea froth offered its bottle lids to the toes of the bodies that were prostrate, as if in reverse worship, as if the sea were desperately searching for gods and thought, poor thing, it had found some. The snow was falling more thickly now, but the bodies seemed unbothered by it. The gone hornwracks left a lemony scent, but no body had the nerves to smell it. The world, or what was left of the world, or what was left of what would have been a world had anybody believed in it, flaked like snowfall. Above the bodies a fly twitched, flustered no doubt by the snow, which fell despite the weather, which though it snowed, and snowed, and snowed, was not all that cold.

Though it feels severe, the other side of abandonment is gradual; abandonment has no clear subject or object – it demolishes both and understands neither. That thought twitched, too, in the air for a while, not thought by anybody in particular. Then the fly found some body on which to land, and bit it. The body that got bit squealed loudly.

To the west of the strip of shore abutted by the dunes the land swept upwards, becoming clifftops. Birdsfoot trefoil grew there, Fin knew, though Fin was not there – not yet. For the time being Fin was still stood in the garden, one foot over the Ha Ha, thinking about a conversation Fin had just had with somebody in the mansion's living-room, somebody who had seemed very young to Fin, with a bloodied sleeve, and amber eyes saddened by something.

Fin had asked the sad amber eyes about being in Fin's future memoir. Fin laughed at the thought of that, now, because it occurred to Fin that Fin was a bit like Willy Wonka. Laughing gave Fin to understand that dreams are sometimes indiscernible from cruelty.

But who the devil was Willy Wonka? Was Willy Wonka even somebody? The name tickled Fin's thoughts with a feathery intimacy, but pointed to nobody.

And who had Fin been talking to in the living-room on the settee? Fin wracked Fin's memory for a name to attach to the sad amber eyes, but found none. It didn't really matter.

The bodies watching the waves welting the beach were meanwhile becoming sleepy. Even the afterparty was over now. Or was anybody up for another round? Somebody claimed never to have stopped. Somebody else announced a pocket full of speed. Another unearthed a Pepsi can from its snowy perch in the sand, having wedged it there to cool, having discovered it earlier in the fridges of Fin's kitchen, which was so pristine it was impossible to tell whether it had never been used or whether it was brand new. The same was true of Fin's mansion in general – it looked old from the outside, the roof was turreted, the front door was studded with great nails and straddled by iron strap hinges, the snow gave it all a quaint sort of feel but the house could easily have been built yesterday. Inside no floorboards creaked, and nothing was dusty.

But then there was that queer ditch that cut between the mansion's garden and the sand dunes. What was that all about? Somebody said it was a relic from a long time ago, when there was no sea to be seen here, and the land was still far longer, and the ditch was to keep the cows away, cows and sometimes madness. Somebody else said that was ridiculous. Why have a ditch and not a wall or a fence? Because a wall or a fence would have destroyed the view, of course, said somebody. But if there wasn't any sea, what was there to be seen? Everybody went quiet then.

Fin had meanwhile come among the tired bodies in silence, having stepped through the dunes, having slid down the ditch's severe side and lain still for a while – it could easily have been hours – before somehow surfacing on the other side. It's not a ditch, said Fin, having overheard the conversation's dregs, it's a Ha Ha – a *Ha Ha*, Fin said again, with emphasis, and the bodies were startled. Then when the bodies had settled, Fin seemed to say *Ha Ha* once more, but this time Fin was again laughing. The laughter came out awkwardly. There was still that agonizing pain in Fin's throat, and now also a great pain in Fin's knees, which Fin must have newly busted upon sliding into the Ha Ha. Fin winced, but the pain was not entirely unpleasant. There was something about it that was comforting.

By the way, said Fin then, pointing, having noticed somebody petting a raw-looking sore, that's not the bite of a fly either. That's the bite of a baby pterosaur.

I shoved Fin gently onwards then, thinking Fin was dizzy from the fall and talking nonsense. I had no reason to act like Fin's bodyguard but I couldn't help but want to protect Fin. I was thin but stronger than I seemed – it had been me who had found Fin collapsed in the Ha Ha, having eventually followed Fin from the living-room into the garden. I had dragged Fin out by the underarms, dozing but still breathing, and though I'd known instinctively that Fin was fine, I had checked Fin's pulses anyway, and when holding two fingers to the skin of Fin's wrists I had noticed a small tattoo in the shape of a tiny coffin, like this ⌒.

I had no idea what the tattoo meant, if it was meant to mean anything, but the way in which the little coffin was empty, containing no body and not buried but just floating on Fin's flesh, like flotsam from a wreck – all this I took to be significant, like a little death instead of a big one. It also just looked pretty.

Fin's body had followed the force of my shove and we were now strolling along the beach together. I was so happy to have Fin's companionship again that I completely forgot all my previous qualms and questions – whether I had ever heard of Fin, how I had come to be here, where I had been before now; such worries all had dissipated. But then when we had gone a fair distance – the sea was fleeing the shore again, appalled by the fake gods it had found there – Fin turned to me with a tired anger in Fin's eyes, as if anger was something Fin found tedious.

I don't know who you think you are, Fin said then, but what I said back there about the pterosaur bite – that was *not* nonsense. The weather overwhelmed whatever Fin said next. Or else I stopped listening. Either way, all I saw was Fin mouthing something.

I don't know who you think you are, Fin had said. That had hurt me, but there was a truth to it. Here I was acting like I was in some way close to Fin, as if there was something special between us, as if I was somehow the same as Fin – as if we shared something.

Ever since I had been a kid, I'd had the feeling that I should have been famous. It wasn't that I *wanted* to be famous, though I would have welcomed the glamour and the trappings, no doubt. But fame for me was never really an ambition. It was more as if fame was the only thing that felt fitting, because it seemed to me that to be famous would be a way of walking out on life without actually walking out on life – or of life walking out on me, and constantly, which is what I always wanted, for life to walk out on me, because in fame the way I could never coincide with the day, or with most things that ever happened to me, would make sense and have a name, so that fame would just be a breathing space for the heavy hard nauseous way in which everything in a life insists on taking on meaning whilst also not meaning anything. It would just be somewhere to put things.

The lives of the legendary are very disposable. Everybody knows this. Fame is both the opposite and not the opposite of disappearing.

The opposite and not the opposite of fame is meanwhile infamy. Infamy is famous shame – shame shown, but not communicated. Infamy is the way the shame I feel *feels* famous, even when it isn't, or is but isn't. It grows into everything except itself.

In silence, without telling anybody, I abandoned the final 'a' of my name around the time I realized I should have been famous, but would not be. A synonym for fame is sometimes *making it*. Alongside the urge to walk out on my life always lived a need to feel as if I was finally doing OK, and not succumbing. To what though? It was difficult to say. Whatever it was had already grown into everything, like wildness, which is sometimes a synonym for abandonment, sometimes a synonym for madness.

The land beyond Fin's garden – beyond the Ha Ha, before the dunes began – was for the most part barren. Styrofoam pebbles scudded the ground like clouds the sky had not loved, and aborted. But there where the land swept upwards from the shore, becoming clifftops, some small flowers grew. Their yellowy petals were weighted with a layering of snow but they wore the weight of it lightly. I knelt down to pet the umbels. Fin watched me. When I asked how it was that flowers grew in such a place, in such weather, Fin said it was because the flowers were vengeful. Vengeful? I said. Yes, Fin replied. Then Fin said the flowers were called *birdsfoot trefoil* or *eggs and bacon* or *lotus corniculatus*. That's a lot of names, I said. Oh only three, Fin answered.

It still wasn't clear to me how flowers of such kind could bloom in winter, but when I asked again Fin just answered – is it? Is it what, I said, confused. Winter, Fin said – maybe it's not, for them. That made me feel nervous. I wanted to change the subject, so I asked how long Fin had lived here.

Fin grinned and pointed seawards. As long as *that's* been here, Fin said, which I found incredibly corny, because when I followed the point of Fin's finger what I saw was the wreck of a cruise ship.

For the life of me, I didn't know how I had not seen it before. There it was, heavier than itself, the hull crushing the rough worn surface of the sea like a bedridden body crushes bedsheets. There it was washed up on the junky rocks, the death of me. Yes, that would have been a good name for her, Fin said suddenly. I looked up sharply. I didn't think that I had spoken aloud and was jolted. Well, what was her name? I asked, surprised too by the way the word *her* went through my mouth, hush-hush, as if it were nothing. What was her name? I repeated, forcing myself to articulate, but Fin just shrugged and said it was an old story. *An Old Story* – was that what the ship was called, or was I once again confused? By then I didn't dare ask Fin.

There she was anyway, her broken body still just afloat. I didn't know how I had not seen her before, but at the same time I did – it was as if she had only appeared the moment Fin pointed to her, after which I couldn't *not* see her, as if the view seawards was one of those Magic Eye images, in which a crazy abstract pattern turns out, if looked at for long enough and in a particular way, to be a picture of reality in 3D. I had never been able to see them as a child, though I had owned a whole book of them – *Magic Eye: A New Way of Looking at the World*, was the title.

I would even venture to say, though it sounds a bit ridiculous, that the reason I could never do Magic Eye puzzles was because I didn't like the idea of revelation. I didn't like the idea of some ultimate *thing* being revealed, destroying what was already there to be seen, trumping the truthfulness of the craziness – or whatever it was that had managed to exist before the revelation.

Either that, or I was terrified of secrets. For secrecy is just like shame, in that it grows into everything, whether half-heartedly or violently, with constant volatility.

It was then, before I had time to ask Fin any more about *An Old Story* and what she had to do with how long Fin had lived here, wherever *here* was, that Fin suggested with a cute wry smile that it was my turn. It didn't occur to me then to question Fin – to point out that Fin had not, as far as I could tell, told a story, so how could it be my turn. I had no idea how old Fin was, I realised, but not because Fin was ageless. Fin's age was obscure in the way my own age felt gone, composed of near and far memories each of which belonged to me, but none of which seemed to go together. I looked seawards and tried to remember if I could swim or not. I couldn't – I couldn't remember if I could swim and that upset me. I looked to Fin for reassurance though I wasn't sure what I thought Fin could offer me. Fin's hair hung in perfect curtains. I touched my own hair anxiously, trying to remember whether it was the kind of hair to be curled by the snow and the party. My body felt floppy. I touched other parts of it. Fin watched with an expression that leapt between fascination and reluctance – as if I were a child that had followed Fin far into a dream, and given Fin no choice but to take responsibility for me.

And yet, I still had the idea of being Fin's bodyguard. On that cliff edge but not because of it, I wanted to protect Fin just as much as I wanted Fin to take care of me – just as much as I wanted, desperately, to be in Fin's future memoir. Or was I already in Fin's memoir? But if I was, if everything that was happening *now* was happening *then*, what was I so desperate about?

Flustered, I looked again at Fin. What was ancient about Fin was the same thing, I now saw, as Fin's air of precocity, the sense that Fin gave of being somebody at once new to life and done with it – the sense Fin gave of being somebody without the words for who they were or where they came from, but not because the answers were secrets; just because those were the wrong questions.

Between our conversation in the living-room and this cliff edge, had I, too, been asking all the wrong questions?

Fin asked if I was ready. It was time to get on with it. It was now or never. I had no real clue what that meant but felt worried anyway. I hate stories, I said, I hate them. I hate the way things happen in them and – I hate everything about them. Fin nodded quickly, neither in agreement nor in sympathy. I was now in a kind of silent rage and also my body was veering, coming back to me as the effects of the ketamine dulled but benumbed, I thought, by the snow and shaking. Just tell me how you ended up here, Fin said then. How can I, I snapped back, when I don't know where *here* is. But you know exactly where you are, said Fin, because ever since then you've always been here. *Where?* I said impatiently. Fin looked back at me with cool lilac eyes. The end, of course, said Fin. I said I thought the end of the world was a children's book, a cliché – and anyway, ever since *when?* Fin smiled, and said I'd misheard slightly.

Whether it was the chemicals or whether it was something else, a wave of nausea washed over me. All of a sudden the worry I'd felt before became a feeling of guiltiness. I wiped my face with my sleeve because I thought I was sweating. My sleeve was covered with blood, I saw when I pulled it away, but had the blood come from my nose when I wiped my face, or was it the blood of somebody else? Now you'll *never* know, Fin cooed. Oh fuck off, I said. Just fuck off. Who do you think *you* are anyway? As I spoke I gathered some snow into my hands and went to chuck it at Fin, but when I let go, nothing happened.

It's not snow, not really, Fin said calmly, answering the question I had not asked yet. It's not what's making you cold either.

What *is* it then? I demanded. Fin shrugged. Who knows, Fin said, maybe it's you – maybe it's you who's snowing.

Well, that was just a little too much for me. Stop it! I shouted. Stop it! Stop saying all these silly corny things! I don't know why I came here. I don't think I've even *heard* of you. What the fuck is that cruise ship doing here and why do you live in that stupid mansion? *Is* it yours? Is what mine, said Fin. *This*, I said, not really knowing myself what I was referring to. I never said it was, Fin said, still calm, still twizzling Fin's fingers in mimicry of a helicopter. Or were Fin's fingers now mimicking a pterosaur? I caught myself getting taken up in it all again, and paused myself. But you did, I said, more slowly. You said that all this was your future memoir and you asked me if I wanted to be in it. Fin grinned. That's true. *What's* true? I said, exasperated, what *bit*? Fin looked at me with what seemed earnest surprise, turned again towards the wreck, and said everything.

An Old Story, if that was after all her name, seemed to me then to smile at Fin. Everything I had felt a moment ago – the anger and guilt and exasperation – became jealousy. And it was then, when I was stood there right at my wits' end, that Fin turned back to me and said I was like her.

What?

You're like her.

Who?

Your sister.

I paused, not knowing what to believe. *Crystal?* You've seen her? I looked around me frantically. She's here? Is she O.K?

No, Fin said simply, in seeming answer to each of my questions. I just mean I can see her in you. You're like her.

I paused, confused, not knowing what to believe.

But after a time I gathered myself, and went to the edge, and sat down and let my feet dangle. The cliff was high, but I felt safe. There was no wind left in the world by then – unless it was the other way round, and there was no world, and Fin was right, the world never was and all that was, was wind, a breeze blowing in nothing. Fin sat beside me and put a hand on my arm, which irritated me. I edged closer to Fin anyhow. The wind or the world growled, then died down again.

She wasn't my sister, I said, eventually.

Not really.

An Old Story

1

Daniel and Fin sit side by side on the cliff edge. The sun is done rising now but already the sky is heavy and grey. The lilac of Fin's eyes has greyed too. Daniel's eyes are still amber.

Out at sea, the wrecked cruise ship heaves. Noxious junk worries her sides; snow has settled atop the junk like Hundreds and Thousands on vanilla ice cream, but with the colours inverted. What Daniel takes to be a gull flees a dreary lowslung cloud, lands on the junk, and pokes around in it.

'I don't really know what to say or where to begin,' says Daniel.

Fin plucks the snowy head of a birds-foot trefoil, flicks the snow off, thumbs the petals of it.

'Tell me as many times as you need. Or if you like, as many times as this.'

'What does *that* mean?' asks Daniel, impatiently.

'Three petals,' Fin shrugs. 'A story for each.'

Daniel winces at the cheesiness of such a suggestion but takes the flower when Fin passes it, swizzles it, thinks.

'It took me three goes at least,' Fin adds, after a bit.

Daniel scowls, looks out to sea, sighs at the sight of the junky waves, which beat against the ship's bruised sides gently, but relentlessly.

'You'll see,' says Fin, and the wrecked ship again heaves, and the gull lets rip a rancid scream, and then, as if something has suddenly come to mind, Daniel begins the first story:—

—Would you believe me if I began by saying my dad was George Michael? You wouldn't, because you think you know who George Michael is, or was, but my dad was also called that. But nobody ever called him that. Everybody called him *Mike* or in Crystal's case *Mika*, though sometimes, when he came home from work, he would open a bill and leave the envelope there on the table, and the torn envelope bore his full name. The name some would have said was his real name. There *George Michael* was anyway, printed on the ripped skin of the envelope.

Beneath the bills would be the day's tabloids, *The Sun* with its heart-sinking headlines and then on page three, the bare breasts.

'Tits,' Crystal would have called them. 'Oh my fucking god, would you just look at them.'

My dad always said he bought *The Sun* for the sport but Crystal, when she came to us, said it was more complicated than that. I thought I knew what she meant but wasn't sure – I didn't understand much about Crystal to begin with. Why would I have done? She came to us like a cloud kicked out of the sky, or like a cloud with no sky to fly in. Her fringe was crimped and her hair was long and I had a feeling she came bearing a secret – that something secretive had borne her to us and our pebbledashed house by the side of the wide road, the world dying in the blanks of her sunglasses.

It was winter. It was me who answered the door to her.

'Hi,' I said.

'Hi,' she said.

She was sixteen but looked at least twenty. I was thirteen but still looked much younger. By her side stood a suitcase made of fabric. Its pattern was flowery, which was funny, I thought, because my dad had paved over the soil in our front yard when my mum left, so the fake fussy flowers on Crystal's case were the first flowers in our yard for a long time. Tied to the handle was a white band with fluorescent green stripes, which made it look like she had come from the airport, though she hadn't.

Somebody else had, some other time. The suitcase was second-hand, Crystal said later.

'Why are you wearing sunglasses?' I wanted to ask, because it was winter, or some version of it.

The weather was already worsening by then. We were waiting for snow as we always were, because at that time my dad worked in the salt mine. If the season was mild and the snow never came, then there wouldn't be any need for the tipper trucks and road gritters, so the salt reserves wouldn't need to be replenished, and then the mine might close for weeks or months at a time. This was long before the miners became archivists – before the salt beds formed from a gone forgotten sea would be repurposed as storage for documents and bank records, celluloid film reels, floppy disks and precious stones. This was before the huge collapses too, the Great Subsidence as they would come to be called, though already there were some of them. The land had been mined for a long time before the mine where my dad worked was built, but mostly haphazardly, creating hazardous cavities that were unseen till they weren't, and the surface of the world was suddenly puckered.

There had always been subsidence of some kind, my dad said, though I think he said that in order to shrug it off – to make out like something was nothing.

In any case, I could never quite believe the sea had once been where the salt now was – I could never get my head round the evaporated fathoms of it.

When the mine closed my dad would take piecework from the elevator factory on the other side of town, or else he would rent out the cab of a lorry, and take jobs delivering goods for stores like Toys 'R' Us. The kind of stores that were always in retail parks back then, where the structures were like glorified warehouses, and in the corner with its own distraught little carpark there was a McDonald's or a Thank God It's Friday's, a TGI Friday's. Either that or he would stay home watching T.V. I'd come downstairs and watch *Neighbours* with him, or not with him exactly – I'd watch *Neighbours* at the same time as him sat at the other end of the settee, and I'd try to guess from the changing shape of his eyes and depth of his sighs what kind of mood he was in, where he was, and whether he was talking to me. Whether he would answer, if I asked him something.

But even when he answered I was never sure, not completely, who was speaking.

That was something *Neighbours* had helped me with – that was something a soap opera had taught me about. What I'd learnt from the way a T.V. character like Henry Ramsay shared a body with the person who played him, Craig McLachlan, without Henry really being Craig McLachlan or Craig completely being

Henry, was that somebody could sometimes be anybody. Henry's body went back to belonging to Craig when Henry was no longer there on the T.V. screen. But where was Craig's body when Henry *was* there on the screen? That part always bothered me. It was like a murder mystery.

When—

> —'Wait,' says Fin. 'What was a murder mystery?
>
> 'The way Craig's body became Henry's in *Neighbours*,' Daniel replies. 'The way a T.V. character can be played by *any*body, actually, without that character ever being anybody but themselves.'
>
> A snowflake touches the end of Daniel's nose; Fin goes to brush it away, then doesn't.
>
> 'But also what happened when Crystal came to stay, I suppose,' says Daniel, before continuing again:—

—When Crystal arrived we were waiting for snow, but the mine was still open and functioning. My dad was back home from work but unbathed, with salt still crusting his eyelashes, which was funny, because it made him look like he had been out in the snow we were constantly hoping would come, and that the non-existent snow had settled on his eyelids. Either that or the tears I never saw him cry – the tears I never imagined him crying – had frozen. We were sat on the settee watching *Home & Away*. *Neighbours* was over but nonetheless, by the time I got up and went to answer the door, Crystal had rung the bell twice, maybe three times.

The last time she rang she kept her finger pressed down on the buzzer till I unslid the chain and stared at her.

'Hi,' I said.

'Hi,' she said, her back to the wide road, her crimped fringe tickling the rim of her sunglasses.

'Are you not going to ask me inside?' she said. 'It's fucking freezing out here.'

I'd never met Crystal in the flesh before then, but her air was completely convincing. I stepped to one side and let her body slip past mine. She walked straight down the hallway to our kitchen, shoved her suitcase next to the fridge, and pulled out a packet of cigarettes.

They were *Luckys*.

Mika—

> —'I'll call my dad *Mika* from now on,' adds Daniel, 'because that was how Crystal always referred to him.'—

—only ever smoked roll-ups. He often claimed he didn't smoke at all. He said his cough was caused by the constant inhalation of salt and sometimes he would even say that while smoking, while the thin paper of the roll-up receded, replaced by grey burn, and I would think how his cigarettes depended on little pieces of ready-prepared paper, each identical in size, each edged with a lickable strip – how tiny items like that were necessary, and came packaged, and existed.

Crystal's *Lucky*s seemed simple by contrast. Firm, and sort of straightforward.

'Can I have one too?' I wanted to ask, and even when I didn't, she offered me one anyway. I felt her watch me slide it from the box through the blue tint of her sunglasses. Then she went over to the window and started to open it, changed her mind, and lit her own cigarette with a pink glittery lighter.

The way she moved made it feel like she already knew our house and its rooms – like she had already lived there, though she hadn't.

Through the wall between the kitchen and the room where Mika still sat unmoved, I could hear the T.V. The adverts mid-way through *Home & Away*. The closing notes of a jingle for something and then before the sunny sagas of *Home & Away* resumed, the start of the advert for the SnowDome, the indoor ski slope where the snow wasn't true and where I'd never been – where Mika wouldn't go out of principle, but also because of the cost of it. How much it would have cost him.

Crystal took a puff on her *Lucky* then tossed her lighter over to me. Its pink glittered body made a fizzy arc between us.

'I suppose you know who I am,' she said. Her voice was different from how it had sounded at the front door. She was speaking now with a voice that didn't quite seem her own, but then I'd never heard Crystal speak before, so how would I have known the difference? How would I have recognized the original?

She smiled slightly, teasingly. 'You wouldn't have let me in otherwise, would you?'

The way she was asking made it feel like an accusation, as if she was tricking me or trying to. I shrugged and took a pull on my own cigarette, coughed but recovered quickly. By then I'd already had plenty of practice smoking the stubbed ends of Mika's skinny roll-ups. I sometimes burnt my eyelashes when lighting them, but that didn't bother me. Sometimes I woke up in the night despising the smell of the smoke and the smudgy touch of its ghost upon me, but only sometimes. Sometimes I stood in front of the long mirror that had once been my mum's, dressed in some of Mika's clothes – a shirt and trousers that swamped me – smoking until I felt nauseous.

I was thirteen but still looked much younger. Crystal was sixteen but looked at least twenty.

But I've said that.

'Well, have you?' Crystal asked between sharp short puffs. Even though she still had her sunglasses on, I could tell she was watching me closely. Her shaded gaze made my body feel weird – fizzy, like the arc of her lighter.

'What?' I said, dazed.

'Have you *heard* of me?'

'Sure,' I said, after a pause, after coming back down to earth or the scuffed lino tiles of our kitchen. Crystal had shifted her query from its first version – she'd asked me if I knew who she was, not if I had *heard* of her – but the difference didn't seem to matter much, so I didn't comment on it. The flesh of her face that wasn't obscured by her shades flushed lavender on account of her cigarette smoke. Her crimped fringe bobbed a bit. She took another abrupt pull on her *Lucky* – Crystal smoked both reluctantly and compulsively, it always seemed to me – shovelled her bum into the corner of our windowsill and exclaimed, 'So you'll know why I'm here then!'

I had an idea why. I knew what Mika had told me – I knew that Mika had had an older sister who had not long ago died on account of the amount of booze she'd poured into her stomach. She had been found sat stiffly at the table, her hand still hugging a glass of something, her forehead kissed by a protrusion of wood on the table's unvarnished surface. I'd imagined the table as being exactly like ours and I'd imagined the ambulance team as having seen that, the hard horrible kiss of death on her forehead, when they'd lifted up her deadened frame, when they'd heaved up the body that once had been hers. We had not gone to the funeral. Mika hadn't seen her for a decade or more before she died – his sister was a half-sister and distant. That made Crystal, who was Mika's half-sister's daughter, something less than my cousin, but what exactly she was to me there wasn't a name for.

'Just think of her as *your* sister,' Mika had shrugged, when I'd asked him how I should refer to her. Then under his breath while exiting the room he had said that she might come to stay with us. He had said that in almost exactly the same way that he had acknowledged my mum's departure three years earlier – hardly, by the yellowy skin of his tobacco-stained teeth, and so quietly I wasn't ultimately sure whether or not I had imagined him saying it.

But here Crystal now was, sat in our house, wearing sunglasses and smoking a *Lucky*.

In those first moments she seemed to me dazzling beyond words, and I was bewildered. Craig McLachlan's ghost might as well have walked through our door, looking for the body that Henry had stolen from him. Except Crystal didn't have a body like Henry Ramsay from *Neighbours*. Crystal's body was Crystal's – she was tall but delicate, strong but contained in a way that feminized her strength and made it seem like grace until it seemed otherwise; it was as if she instinctively knew how to cultivate each gesture she made as though doing so was like curling an eyelash or manicuring a nail. Her body was nothing like I remembered my mum's being, slumped and hurried, her skin curdled from years of Mika's smoke and worrying.

I didn't think I'd ever seen a girl like Crystal before – or a woman, since that's what she was nearly.

'I have an idea, *naturally*,' I said, after a brief gasp of silence, in delayed answer to her suggestion that I knew why she was here now – and it was true, I did have an idea, but I had no clue then what Crystal's visit would so strangely coincide with or where her influence would lead me, and in a way I still don't. I just know now, though I didn't know then, that she would leave me along with the ground beneath my feet, suddenly, massively, devastatingly.

Crystal snorted at my high-falutin voice – though I was only trying to talk like she had just done – then said in the same fake snapped tone, 'Yes, *naturally*.'

She tapped her ash out on the skull of one of the figurines that stood on the windowsill her bum was squeezed into. The figurines were Mika's, not my mum's as might have been expected, and the one Crystal had eliminated her cigarette upon was Mika's favourite. It was Princess Diana, dressed like a mermaid. I stared at the vandalized figurine. From her head cascaded miniature curls of ash. Then Crystal cupped her hand gently over her belly, exhaled, and announced that she needed the toilet.

I stood quietly by the door while she went, listening for the tinkling of her urine.—

—Here Daniel pauses. Fin is conspicuously fidgeting.

'What is it?' asks Daniel who, having been so hesitant to begin, is now keen to get on with things.

'I don't think I know who Princess Diana is,' Fin says. In the distance, beyond the battered ship, the cusp of a faint crescent moon hooks onto the cusp of a second moon. Both moons will soon leave the sky, first one and then the other.

Daniel looks disbelievingly at Fin, then grins.

'A friend of George Michael,' says Daniel, before continuing:—

—Mika barely commented on Crystal's arrival. He might have nodded at her. He accepted her presence or seemed to at least, but he never told me how to arrange things in our house in order to accommodate her visit. His silence was as unnerving as it was unsurprising and I felt embarrassed and blankly ashamed, because Crystal was a guest after all. Mika never mentioned how long she'd be staying or whether her visit was temporary or permanent. Nor did Crystal seem interested in explaining – but then Crystal was never very interested in anything definite. To begin with all I really knew for sure was that she had come to live with us for a while, and that who she was had something to do with the past and somehow by association our flowerless front yard, and that the best way to think of her was as Mika had suggested – as the older sibling I had never had. Somebody I could talk to without worrying about the hard heavy weightlessness of my words and whether I should have said them at all, because there wasn't anything you couldn't say to Crystal.

There wasn't anything that could uncrimp her fringe or kill the grin her jaw was always about to sneak into. She was exciting.

Of course she was.

Where we lived, in a place that wasn't a city or even the edge of one, but something once known as an *overspill town*, built up from the scraps of a scattering of villages when the city where Mika had been born had cleared out the last slums at its centre, and sent the people who'd lived in them to work down the mine or in the newly-built elevator factory – I'd always thought it was funny, how our town was flanked by a mine and a mechanical lift factory, and that the rooms of the mine were underground in a way that was both different and similar to the spaces created in the factory, where they made machines to transport bodies elsewhere, up up and away – there, where we lived, people were people. People were just who they were, I mean, and most were too consumed by work or the possibility of its loss to have time or money to be anything other than what they appeared to be.—

—'But you said that Mika wasn't always himself,' Fin says. 'You said somebody could sometimes be *any*body.'

Daniel briefly considers the significance of this inconsistency, shrugs, continues:—

—It was a small labouring town in the North. The name doesn't matter – I doubt you'd ever have heard of it. Most of the houses were pebbledashed like ours and most were still owned by the government. Nobody commuted. Nobody ever seemed to get round to leaving, though somehow my mum had. Since she'd gone Mika had mostly kept to himself and I'd followed suit – I rarely went over to friends' or had friends around. I had few friends in those days anyway. At school, a building too big, or too optimistic, for the number of kids it ever accommodated, I was too boyish for the girls and too soft for the boys, who accepted my presence when they needed a left foot for football but objected to my lopped-off hair and unspoken unavailability when it came to games of spin-the-bottle. Increasingly I just skipped school. I roamed around town shoplifting sweet little nothings and brollies, even when there was nothing coming down from the sky for them to protect me from. I sat on the settee watching T.V. or re-reading old copies of *The Sun*, which Mika kept stashed in a corner of the kitchen, behind the door, beneath a chipped and disfavoured figurine.

So though part of me wanted to tell the whole world, I told nobody about Crystal's arrival. There was nobody really to tell, so there was nobody to accuse me of exaggerating had I described her clothes and the things that she claimed – nobody to accuse me of having a manic imagination or being feral in the head if not body.

But I did start wearing her sunglasses.—

—'Which,' says Fin, interrupting again, 'is how you came to believe you were famous. Right?'

'How I came to feel I should have been, you mean,' says Daniel, taken aback by Fin's intuition. *Did I already tell Fin this about me?* Daniel thinks, before quickly insisting, 'There's a difference.'

The junky sea fizzes friskily. Fin blinks, as if momentarily confused. The creature Daniel previously took to be a gull has disappeared – or else it has dipped beneath the jagged rim of the cliff, unseen by Fin and Daniel for the time being.

'Yes,' says Fin. 'Sorry. I was getting mixed up.'

'With what? What were you getting mixed up with?'

'With my own story, of course,' Fin replies, matter-of-factly, as if it's the most obvious thing in the world. 'With my own reasons for being here.'

But you haven't told me your story, Daniel thinks. But nor does Daniel want to stop at this point, and so, though Daniel is still bristling with curiosity, like the brittle air is busy with snowflakes and shampoo microbeads, Daniel presses on with the story of Crystal's sunglasses:—

—She gave them to me the day after she arrived, though *gave* isn't really the word for it.

I'd decided Crystal should have my bedroom at night on account of the fact that she was older, and I didn't mind sleeping downstairs on the settee where I could doze off to the dimmed chatter of the T.V., and if I wanted to I could keep my Reeboks on. The Reeboks were freebies from one of Mika's lorry jobs and I would have kept them on all the time if I could, but I couldn't keep them on under my duvet, which was turquoise and everywhere printed with fish so that being under it was like being under the deep sea that had once been where we lived. The same sea that had crept across the sand dunes and sandbanks of the huge sunken basin in the supercontinent we were once part of, only then to evaporate, leaving the salt that Mika now mined behind. The sea whose existence I never could fathom and—

> —'I know I'm drifting,' adds Daniel, 'but this is important, believe me.'—

—the same sea that would soon make itself felt unimaginably, when the collapses that had long sporadically happened in and around our town happened massively.

By the time of Crystal's arrival, looking back from where I am now, wherever I am now, there was already evidence of their intensification. There was already an increase in the number of sags in the ground caused by the collapse of an abandoned room of an old mine roughshod constructed before the modern one was built, and there were the ditches. The sinkholes and hollows and troughlike depressions. Those were caused by a technique known as wild brine pumping – I was never sure what exactly was *wild* about it, what the word *wild* meant when coupled with *brine pumping*—

> —'Wild just means *outrageous*,' Fin says. 'When something takes up more space than it should do.'—

—but I knew that it wasn't supposed to happen anymore and I knew it involved dissolving the saliferous deposits and flushing them out, softening the ground in the process. A ditch that seemed at first glance to be natural, a given aspect of the landscape, would turn out to be there because of subsidence.

Most of the ditches in the fields across from our house were man-made, artificial. Sometimes they appeared in gullies between buildings too, and occasionally beneath them. A hollow or trough just abrubtly materialized, unpredictably and years after extraction, sometimes at a great distance to where the work had been done.

Ordinariness is always precarious

Where the ditches appeared was unpredictable, I mean. Or at least, it was for a time, before unpredictability became ordinary.

But then ordinariness has always been unpredictable for some people, Crystal would have said. Or no, she would have said that ordinariness is always precarious.

But I haven't said enough about Crystal yet for the things she said or would have said to make sense.

Mika said salt was the most untrustworthy substance in the world, but that the world would be nothing without it. There wouldn't *be* a world, not as we knew it. Salt lowered the melting point of snow when there was snow, kept the roads open, kept stuff circulating. Salt put food on our table as well as making it tasty and though Mika was not religious he'd once told me there was salt in holy water, a small sacred sprinkling of it. 'Do you know there's even salt in plastic?' he would say, during the times when he was speaking, his moustache twinkling with milk from his cereal bowl, his spoon swinging like a confused compass point between my hovering torso and the increasing mess of our kitchen. Our kitchen became messier and messier in the years after my mum left. Every now and then I would take it upon myself to re-introduce order, but often excessively, so that every Tupperware we ever owned was labelled in permanent marker with words that soon lost their reference, and became nonsensical, and our cupboards were full of tubs that boldly announced they contained teabags or instant coffee or nuts – Mika loved nuts, ate big salty piles of them – when really they contained leftovers, or were empty.

There was plastic in salt too by then, of course, microplastics in sea salt, but Mika wasn't concerned with that. —

> —'But you were saying how you came to wear Crystal's sunglasses,' Fin says.
> 'Yes,' says Daniel, 'I'm getting there.'—

—Crystal's sunglasses, it goes without saying, were made of plastic, though to me they looked snazzy, and expensive.

From my bedroom window you could see out over our front yard and the liver-spotted roof of a bus shelter, across the wide road to the creasing fields and within them, the entrance to the salt mine, which Mika always called the *rockpit*. A hoarding announced the existence of it, because above ground there was nothing much to it – just the staggered salt piles and shoots like covered slides, the office trailers constructed from corrugated iron and then the clubhouse, where they sometimes held parties.

When I came upstairs in the morning to see if Crystal was still there – there was no reason for her not to be but nonetheless, I couldn't quite believe that she would be – she was stood by my window, smoking again. Either she hadn't taken her sunglasses off since arriving or I was yet to see her without them. She was wearing a pair of oversized pyjamas. They looked like men's pyjamas to me, though men's clothes on Crystal's body looked different to men's clothes on my body. On her the PJs were both alien and luxurious. The elasticated bottoms practically dripped off her hips while the shirt clung delicately, maybe desperately, to the sheer bones of her shoulders. She didn't seem to sense my presence at the door, so I coughed to draw her attention and also on account of her cigarette – what I mean is I made out that my cough was caused by the smoke, when really I just wanted Crystal's attention. Why wouldn't I have done?

'Hi,' she said, without turning to look at me.

'Hi,' I said, and then quickly, because by then I'd gathered the courage to ask, had already made up my mind to before I'd come upstairs, 'Why are you wearing *sunglasses?*'

It was early and though the sun was done coming up, the sky was still grey and cumbersome, so I switched the light on. Crystal shuddered extravagantly and put out her cigarette – on the sill itself this time. Then she sat back down on my bed, crossed her long legs on top of my duvet, and slid the sunglasses off.

I looked at her.

Her right eye was fine, but her left eye was bruised and sore-looking. The lid of it was purpling and swollen, so much so that it must have obscured her vision. It must have hurt a lot too, I thought, but without knowing why I knew not to ask her what had happened.

I sat down on the bed beside Crystal. Her sunglasses perched on a swell in the duvet between us. I let my fingers move to them but didn't dare pick them up – I just touched the curved end of an arm, as if I was comforting them.

My bedroom in that house was small and made smaller on account of the walls being all collaged with clippings. Not with posters as might have been expected for somebody my age, but stories from *The Sun* that had caught my imagination, diagrams for old household items and outlandish furniture we'd never have owned, plus pictures of distant solar systems. Crystal's uncovered eyes surveyed the walls and came to rest on one of the headlines. It was the headline I was most obsessed with, the one that read:

I DECDIED TO BECOME BLIND BUT I WOULD NOT SAY I HAD A CHOICE

and after it, an exclamation mark—

!

—The exclamation mark was what most fascinated me about the headline. It didn't seem to add anything to the sentence it ended – it didn't seem to express anything, I mean, but there it was anyway, exclaiming.

'That's how it happened,' Crystal said, her eyes still steadied on the bold font of the headline, her fringe still crimped despite a night's sleep, and I laughed out loud because I thought she was joking.

But she wasn't joking.

'I'm not fucking joking,' she said, and I thought then that she was going to cry, but instead she just picked at her toenails. Her toenails were painted multiple colours, which both astonished and delighted me. One was a turquoise that matched the watery parts of my duvet, one was orange, another was the same glittery pink of her cigarette lighter and the rest were a grey kind of lilac, like the sky left behind by the sunrise. The colour of Crystal's unglassed eyes was sometimes grey, sometimes lilac. I knew that now – now that she had taken her sunglasses off.

'I'm not joking,' Crystal repeated, slowly turning her bruised eye towards me. 'That's how *this* happened.'

'OK,' I said, because I didn't know what to do with what she had said – I didn't know how it could possibly be true or what she meant, but I also couldn't think of any way of disproving her. And it was morning, so I was hungry.

'I'm hungry too,' Crystal whispered, and I flinched a little.

I skipped quickly over the fact that she'd seemed to know what I was thinking and started to tell her what we had downstairs to eat, but Crystal didn't want any of it. She shook her head slightly but firmly, stood up, snatched the sunglasses from their perch on the duvet and shoved them into my lap – just like that, Crystal's sunglasses became mine – then announced that what she wanted to eat, the only thing in the world she could possibly eat, was Chicken McNuggets dipped in ketchup.

'But I've got school,' I said, unconvincingly. Already by then, as I've already said, I'd begun skipping lessons or sneaking in during the lunch break. Mika never said anything that suggested he'd noticed, or if he had that he could have cared less, but then – increasingly, ever since my mum left – Mika never said anything about anything.

'Go after,' Crystal shrugged, and I nodded quickly.

There was a McDonald's not far away. Not one of those restaurants that serviced retail park customers, but a drive-in by the side of the same wide road that we lived on. The road climbed a long slouchy slope – it wasn't quite a hill though it might have liked to have been – and eventually the pebbledashed houses like ours that lined it fell away, and there were empty plots marked out with ticker tape, beyond them the fields, and then the road reached a dull peak and that's where the McDonald's was.

It wasn't obvious why that was a good spot for a restaurant. Probably it had been built there in anticipation of the road's future development, but that future had lapsed before it ever arrived. That was another funny thing about our town, if *town* was even the right word for it. In the beginning, when people had first moved there, it had been unfinished in a way that promised futurity, without pubs or supermarkets but only temporarily or for the time being – but now it was unfinished in a different sense. Now its incompletion seemed permanent and constantly encroaching, a force almost like gravity. The buses to the city were increasingly irregular, and increasingly prohibitively expensive. The salt extraction meant to sustain the town economically made its terrain increasingly, if indecipherably, unstable. I still hoped for snow anyway. I still poured too much salt on my food and I still loved McDonald's.

Of course I did.

The billboards that lined the upper part of the road were unused and mostly dilapidated. Wildflowers clung to their sides like Crystal's pyjamas had clung to her shoulders, but Crystal wasn't wearing her pyjamas now. Before we'd left the house to make our way to the restaurant for breakfast she'd dressed again in yesterday's clothes – jeans and a grey sweatshirt and over it, an extremely tight denim gilet. On her feet she wore white sports socks shoved into high red heels. It seemed to me that Crystal walked in her heels as easily I walked in my Reeboks, except that the heels made Crystal walk differently, with her hips leading, leaving me completely baffled as to how she kept her balance so effortlessly. Otherwise everything about her was exactly the same as it had been the day before, expect now I was wearing her sunglasses.

I was thrilled to be wearing her sunglasses.

It was a fine day. It was winter but the weather wasn't especially cold—

> —'Because the weather was already worsening?' Fin asks. 'Or because you didn't feel the cold? You said Crystal said it was freezing.'
>
> 'I know,' says Daniel, increasingly irritated by Fin's querying, though also a little intimidated. *Or is it that Fin is attempting to help me?* Daniel thinks. *Is Fin somehow telling* me *something?*
>
> 'I guess Crystal did feel the cold excessively,' Daniel says. 'But then I did too, in some ways.'—

—so I was wearing a T-shirt but mittens too, because no matter what the weather was doing, my extremities always seemed to be freezing. Crystal's eyebrows had risen at the sight of the mittens when she'd seen me pull them on at the door, but I hadn't thought much of that. Not coming from her. The sky we stepped under was huge and swirling. Crystal didn't seem to want to talk as we walked, so I didn't comment on the single lingering crescent moon, and I didn't worry her with questions about how long she'd be staying, and I didn't ask her about her poorly eye. But I did consider what she'd said about it, what she'd meant when she pointed to the headline from *The Sun* cellotaped to my wall:

I DECIDED TO BECOME BLIND BUT I WOULD NOT SAY I HAD A CHOICE!

'That's how it happened,' Crystal had said.

I didn't know what she had meant by that or why she'd decided to hand her sunglasses over to me in that moment. What was it that had passed between us? I wondered. The headline referred to a story – I knew it by heart, almost – about a woman who had always believed she should have been blind, but whose vision was just fine, and so in order to become blind, in order to become what she felt she ought to have been, she had poured bleach into her eyes on purpose. The story didn't mention the name of the brand, but I always thought it must have been *Kleos*—

— 'Fame,' Fin nods. '*Kleos* means fame.' —

—which was the name of the cleaning brand I usually chose from the shelves whenever Mika gave me money to do a shop, and the same brand that made our detergent, which was another substance whose existence depended upon salt, because detergent was made by splitting salt into its component parts, sodium and chloride. It was as if – this was how I thought about the story in *The Sun*, which I felt a mysterious affinity with, even though I myself had no desire to be blind and definitely no feeling that I should have been – it was as if there was something about the woman that the truth couldn't see, and so she had had to correct it.

She herself had had to correct the truth by going blind on purpose.

Or – and this was my slightly improved version, the explanation I was best pleased with – it was like the world the woman saw couldn't see her in turn, and so she had had to reverse things, to make up for that inconsistency, that little gap or difference.

That was how I thought about it, but no matter how much I thought about it, the headline was still a conundrum. I didn't know why *I* was so drawn to it, and I didn't know, not for the life of me, why Crystal would have said that was what had happened to her. It seemed clear to me that that was not what had happened, but at the same time I guessed it could have done. The woman in the story had poured bleach into her eyes, after all, so it wasn't impossible, so it was possible – this was what I was thinking about as we passed the last empty plots by the side of the wide road and approached the low bungalow structure that housed the McDonald's – it was possible that what Crystal was pointing to when she'd pointed at the headline taped to my wall, what she was talking about, was just the feeling that she *could have* done that.

She felt like she could have poured bleached into her eyes.

I felt chuffed with my conclusion. I felt close to Crystal even though I had so little to go on, even though really I hardly knew her.

We crossed over to where the restaurant was. The building was squat and stubby beneath the swirly sky. Its neon sign was losing its life or maybe its mind – that's what I thought looking at it through Crystal's shades anyway. Half of the great *M* was unlit, while the other half sizzled bluely. No cars made their way through the drive-in, but then no cars had past us on our way up the road either. That wasn't unusual. Crystal had been smoking another *Lucky* as we walked. She put it out now in a casual stamp and I made a mental note to remember the way she swivelled her foot on it, so that its grey burn ground into the slabs that flanked the entrance to the McDonald's.

The *Lucky* died, and I pushed the glass doors of the restaurant open.

'I love it here,' Crystal declared, before the doors had hardly closed behind us.

There were McDonald's everywhere. When Crystal said *here* she could have meant anywhere.

And then, both flatly and profoundly, as if there was no contradiction at all with what she'd said earlier—

'I'm vegetarian.'

'But you said you wanted Chicken McNuggets,' I said, tugging my mittens off, keeping her sunglasses on.

She shrugged.

I ordered.

The till vendor who served us was the son of a foreman at the elevator factory, who was the brother-in-law of a foreman of the salt mine. I knew of this convoluted connection because of Mika, who had a vendetta against anybody who made something of themselves as far as I could tell, and especially anybody who was a foreman. I didn't know the till vendor's name, but I knew that he had recently finished school so was only a few years older than Crystal, though he looked younger. She looked the age he should have looked.

His hair beneath the unwincing light of the McDonald's was glossy and perfectly curtained. He looked like a boy from a boyband, I thought – from one of those groups that, unlike George Michael in *Wham!*, couldn't sing and couldn't dance, but that girls all over the world still threw their knickers at. So many of those groups were being manufactured back then – packaged, like dainty cigarette papers. His skin was darker than either Crystal's or mine, though at the time I thought nothing of that. Many of the kids in my school weren't white; white wasn't the ordinary where we lived, though in another way it was of course.

It would be a while still before I understood my whiteness for what it was, an ability to keep experiencing the end of the world metaphorically, at a distance, as opposed to literally.

But that's not to say the ground was ever very stable.

But I'm getting ahead of myself.

Crystal kept her poorly eye fixed on the foreman's son while he fetched our order from the racks behind the counter. I kept her sunglasses on. When our food came, he slid the loaded tray towards where I stood and waved his hand when I sank mine for money. Crystal had made no suggestion of intending to pay. The floor of the restaurant had recently been cleaned. We slipped over to a booth near to the gates that separated the main restaurant off from children's party area. No party was happening at that time of the morning. We were the restaurant's only customers.

'Who was *that*?' Crystal asked, when we were sitting down.

I clicked open the Styrofoam clamshell containing my fish burger, my Filet O' Fish, and told her pretty much what I've just told you.

'He's sexy,' she cooed. Then she asked me what his name was. When I replied that I didn't know his name, Crystal told me not to be stupid. His name had been right there on his namebadge. Had I not seen?

'No,' I said, confused but not wanting to admit it.

'Can you see *anything* wearing those sunglasses?' Crystal said, which was once again rich, I thought, coming from her, though I didn't say so.

She dipped a Chicken McNugget into a ripped sachet of tomato ketchup, licked and sucked at the nugget, then placed what was left of it, soggy and shrivelled, on a carefully unfolded paper napkin. I stared at the sucked McNugget. Maybe it was fair for Crystal to call herself vegetarian. Maybe she'd told the truth after all. There was something about the immediacy of her compulsions – even if they were conflicted, or maybe because they were – that was fascinating to me, and entrancing. To me it seemed like Crystal did exactly what she wanted, though there was also an absence in her, and a shrill sadness. I understood that right from the beginning, maybe because I recognised in her something I'd already seen, too close-up to make that much sense of, in Mika – and maybe in myself too. It wasn't just grief – it wasn't just her mum's dying, I mean – or it was but the grief was for something amiss, something that might never have existed, though I couldn't necessarily have named any of this at the time, not directly, not for the life of me.

Then – just like that – her shrill sadness would be gone again anyway, and her body was again organised by everyday objects and surfaces, by the McDonald's tabletop and slippery floor tiles, and Crystal's hard pointy elbows and heeled feet upon them.

She tilted her head to look past me at Ace – I couldn't believe that was really his name, *Ace*, was sure I'd never heard of anybody called that before – then she snatched at a second McNugget.—

—Here Daniel again pauses. Fin is now smiling widely.

'What?' asks Daniel. 'What's so funny?'

'Nothing,' Fin replies, still smiling. 'It's

just interesting listening to this version of Crystal.'

'What do you mean, this *version*?' says Daniel, whose amber eyes are now burning up, unless it's just the sight of the sun reflected. The sky where Fin and Daniel are is grey and still fluffy with snow, but the sun is red and piercing. Only one crescent moon is visible now – just about. Its bum sits cheekily on the funnel of the wrecked ship, which every now and then creaks hopefully, as if recovering. The winged creature is again zooming and diving – its broad wings are vividly feathered; its tail looks like the bow of an arrow. *Gulls don't have tails though*, Daniel thinks.

Fin has meanwhile begun humming something – some song or other – that Daniel doesn't recognise. The notes seem just a tad flat, off-key, strained and a fraction out of tune. *That should surprise me*, Daniel thinks, remembering the piano in Fin's living room, *but it doesn't somehow.* Then, immediately having thought this, Daniel remembers having no memory of ever having heard of Fin, let alone knowing what Fin is or was famous for.

I don't even know for sure if Fin is famous at all, Daniel thinks, watching the winged creature deftly skim a cloud. *For some reason I'm still here though. For some reason I'm still sat here on this cliff edge, telling Fin about Mika and McDonald's and Crystal.*

'What do you mean, this version of Crystal?' Daniel asks again, after Fin's humming has dissipated.

'Just keep going,' Fin replies, 'and I think you'll start to understand. You'll figure it out, eventually.'—

—Probably, I assumed, because of Ace, possibly because Crystal really did love the taste of unbitten-McNuggets-dipped-in-ketchup, this breakfast trip up to the McDonald's became our ritual. For a while at least. It didn't last but it seemed like it might. Each morning as we made our way up the road to the squat McDonald's with its sizzling blue M, we walked in silence – Crystal in her high red heels, me in my Reeboks. I came to like the quiet that hung between us. Mika's silences troubled me, but with Crystal I felt comfortable. I didn't mind us not speaking for a while, perhaps because I understood our silences would come to pass, whereas with Mika it always seemed like a particular silence might be the last – like this time, he would never come back from it.

Since she'd arrived I had seen Crystal try, a number of times, to talk to him, but he'd just looked at her like she wasn't there, frowned, and turned the T.V. on. She would stand there a moment, her face freshly startled by his rebuff. Then her face would glaze over and she would huff off again.

As we walked together up to the McDonald's, I could always tell that Crystal had things on her mind, and also that the landscape intrigued her, though she never asked why it was the way that it was. She never wondered aloud why the pebbledashed houses abrubtly stopped or what the plots were waiting for, why so few cars went up and down our road despite its size – you knew from its width that it should have been a thoroughfare – so the awkward gawky terrain of our town and the surrounding landscape remained untouched by my explanations. The early morning yawning sun would try its best to enlighten it, just as the winter tried its best to be wintry, sometimes succeeding in depositing a frosty topping on the overgrown grass in the plots and on the ditchy fields beyond them. When the frosty topping and morning light combined it looked like the world had been covered in clingfilm, or shrinkwrap – like the plots had been packed up like sandwiches, or protected from disturbance like murder scenes, or wrapped like a baby born prematurely and secured from the air's brittle poisons.

Either that or the ground had been heavily salted, even though there was no snow upon it.

I never commented on these things as we walked up the road, but I did make a point of keeping my head tilted towards the single lingering moon, of keeping my tinted eyes bent upon it.

'Hhhhm,' I hummed sometimes, regarding the moon's shape. *Hhhhm* didn't count as saying something.

Inside the McDonald's our silences shifted. Crystal would begin talking about what she fancied eating immediately after entering, and I'd offer my thoughts on her list of choices. She always ended up ordering McNuggets. I always ordered a Filet O' Fish. 'Fish is *disgusting*,' Crystal hissed every time. 'Fish flesh has millions of little pieces of plastic swimming in it,' she'd say, and I'd shrug and say that salt did too – so did the salt we sucked off our fingers each morning. We always ordered a small portion of fries each. I liked the sound of the papery wrapper against the slim greasy strips of potato and the way the salt granules collected at the bottom of the bag, as if they knew one another, as if they were siblings. We never paid. Ace waved his hand every time, so I never once, on any of our trips to McDonald's during those first weeks of Crystal's visit, had to make use of the coins I'd kept back from the money that Mika gave me to do our shops.

Before she'd gone my mum had done our shopping, though sometimes, when Mika forgot her birthday or remembered at the last moment, he would press a folded fiver into my reluctant palm and send me off to the newsagents to buy her a card and present for him.

I'd hated doing that, but not for my mum's sake – I hated it because it meant Mika assumed I would know what a woman would want to get, even if it also meant that he was recruiting me to his masculinity, making me make up for his manly, unmanly obliviousness.

After we'd sat down in the booth with our food, we would talk about all sorts and anything. I say that but Crystal probably thought we were talking about nothing, though to me it felt like we talked about everything. By about our fifth breakfast trip – I wouldn't have believed it was only the fifth, because already by then it seemed to me as if Crystal had been staying with us for ages, and that life before her had been but a lacklustre untalented karaoke version of the life that might be possible with Crystal in it – I decided it was about time that I told her about my knowledge of the Universe.

Crystal always sat so she see could past me to Ace, which meant that behind her sat the statue of Ronald McDonald, whose body had been caught out by an avalanche or volcanic eruption and frozen in that form forever. His eyes were unhappy and astonished like Crystal's poorly eye – her eye had hardly healed since she'd turned up at our house – while his gloved hand was cheerily waving. Outside the McDonald's there was another Ronald, also a statue but not a duplicate. That Ronald was sat on a bench with his foot propped coquettishly up on his knee. Somebody, not me, had left a milkshake nested between his legs next to his crotch and birds had shat happily upon his blue rinse. I thought now of that other Ronald sat outside alone, and felt bad. I wondered if Crystal had noticed him too, and whether seeing him might have made her think of her mum and the way she had died – how her lifeless body had been found at the kitchen table, sat stiffly.

'Crystal,' I said, very seriously.

'Yeah love?'

I blushed at the *love* and waited for her to take her first lick of dipped chicken. I'd meant to speak slowly, with confidence. It didn't quite come out that way, but then nothing much did when I tried to speak.

'On the other world,' I said, suddenly unsure, suddenly full of myself – 'On the other world there is only *one* moon.'

Crystal's unmatching eyes didn't move, so I said what I'd said again with extra emphasis.

She stuck a salty fry in her ear and looked at me. 'That sentence doesn't make any sense.'

The fry fell from her ear.

'Yeah it does,' I said, rolling my eyes like I'd seen Crystal do. '*And—*'

'Hhhhm?' There was a kindness in her *hhhhm*, even an encouragement.

'Everything else there is exactly the same as it is here, except nobody *there* knows there's another world.'

Crystal said nothing, just stared at me.

'Only *we* know that,' I added, worried I wasn't being clear. 'Only *we* know that there's another world exactly like our own, or *almost* exactly like it.'

'Alright,' she said.

'Great,' I said, because I didn't know what else to say.

And then I said—

'Because we have two moons.'

'You mentioned.'

'Yeah. We have two moons whereas they have one moon but everything else there is exactly the same as here, except for the fact that nobody *there* knows about the existence of this world.'

'OK,' she said. 'That's quite a theory.'

I munched on a mouthful of Filet-O-Fish. The lettuce leaf was limp and delicious, like always. The tartare sauce, which I took to be lemony mayo, glooped exuberantly from the bun's squashy edges. Crystal was sucking another McNugget and scowling. Her eyebrows were finer than they'd been the first time I'd seen them, when they'd floated like lovely chubby slugs above the frames of the same shades I was now wearing. She must have been plucking them furiously.

'Is that why the weather's losing it?' she said between sucks. 'Because we have two moons? It's nothing to do with the environment or climate change or – who knows – the end of the world?'

She smiled a tiny wry smile when she said that. Everybody where we lived was always worrying about the weather – everybody was always waiting for the winter to be itself, to deliver what was needed to keep the keep the mine open, things ticking over, plates spinning, evenings to lean into with T.V. shows to sink into – but nobody ever talked about *climate change*. Not at that point.

'It's all to do with this second moon of yours?'

'It's not a *theory*,' I said sulkily, ignoring the second part of what she'd said.

'No?'

'No.'

And then Crystal just said—

'Shall I tell you why I was sent here?'

I took a quick startled breath then. I thought we'd already agreed I had an idea why she was here, but I was pleased that she wanted to expand for me. I was annoyed she'd passed so quickly over what I'd said, given its significance and enormity, but I was glad that she wanted to share something with me. I was more than glad – I was delighted that Crystal wanted to confide in me. Why wouldn't I have been?

'Sure,' I said.

'I killed somebody.'

Her voice sounded bored, almost exasperated. There was no kindness in her tone now, only a low muttering frustration.

'Yeah. I'm a murderer.'

A little tick of ketchup had leapt from a McNugget to the grey sleeve of her sweatshirt. She noticed it and tried to lick the tick off, lifting her sleeve to her out-stuck tongue, its tip curled perfectly.

Then she rubbed at the tongued mark with a napkin.

'I don't believe you,' I said, watching her.

'No,' she said, still rubbing. 'Nobody does. Nobody did. Who would do? Little girls are murdered, not murderers. Little girls should be seen and not heard!'

It seemed strange to me that Crystal would refer to herself as a *little girl*, because to me she didn't seem like one. Or maybe she was only half-including herself in the term – maybe she was just repeating what somebody else had said of her.

'That's why they sent me to this shithole instead of to prison.'

I realised then I knew almost nothing about where Crystal had been before she'd arrived at our house, what she'd been doing since her mum died – it must have been at least a few months ago now – or who she had lived with during that time. Had she been going to school somewhere? She hadn't talked about school at all since she'd come to us. I'd just assumed that she must have been done with it. Maybe she was waiting for Mika to say something about the way she spent her days – maybe she was hoping he'd eventually notice her. Maybe I was hoping the same too.

'Everybody thought I was crazy for saying it. Or – let me see – just making things up?'

She was still fixated on that little tick of ketchup.

'Why would you make something like that up?'

'Why do you think?'

'*I* dunno.'

Crystal sat back in her chair and stared at me. Her stare was like the static caused by the plastic McDonald's chairs, sharp and electrifying. Into my head popped the question of how much time had passed after Crystal's mum died before the ambulance had come for her. How long had her mum's body been bent at the table, her hand still hugging a glass of something? How long had it been before Crystal had called for help – how long had she moved through the rooms of her house with her mum's stopped body left literally for dead like that? I wondered why I hadn't wondered about any of this before, then wondered why I was wondering. I didn't think that Crystal could have done something like that, and anyway, how could you murder somebody who was dead already?

Crystal was meanwhile still waiting for me to come up with some kind of answer to her question.

I didn't.

'To get attention, duh,' she said.

In between the instances of her speech it seemed to me that Crystal did little frittering sighs, as if what she was saying was wearisome to explain. This annoyed me, because I had tried to talk to her about something important and she had trumped me. I suspected her of making fun of me. Or was she telling the truth? Was Crystal really confiding in me? But if she was, what bit was true – the bit about her killing somebody or the bit about nobody believing her? It could have been true that nobody had believed her, without it being true that she had actually killed somebody, in which case it was possible that she was lying without lying completely.

Or else the whole story could have been true, unless it was all just a story.

To my right, Ace scrubbed a tabletop that didn't need scrubbing. He was doing it to be nearer to Crystal, I thought. Ace was what the girls in my school would have called *fit*, though Crystal hadn't used that word for him – Crystal had called him *sexy*. I felt jealousy form a fist in my belly, which felt like a hit of adrenaline.

'You came here because your mum died,' I said. 'She died because she drank too much.'

I felt almost as thrilled by my cruelty as I felt thrilled by wearing Crystal's sunglasses – and maybe that was exactly what she wanted. Maybe that was what Crystal wanted me to feel.

'Also,' I added after a bit, my fingers picking at the frayed lip of the Formica tabletop, my jaws still churning flakes of Filet-O'Fish, 'You wouldn't have been sent to prison. *You'd* have been sent to a detention centre.'

'Yeah?' she said.

'Yeah,' I said.

But Crystal's attention was already elsewhere. She had finished fussing with the tick of ketchup and was now resting her chin in the palm of her hand, gazing over to where Ace was working. Her good eye was fully made up, with lashes thick with mascara, which clung in clumps to the tiny curved hairs in the same way salt crusted Mika's when he came home from the rockpit. I wondered if Mika knew where I was, and if he cared. I felt bad for having spoken so bluntly of Crystal's mum and wondered, suddenly, where my own was. I hardly heard from her. Sometimes she telephoned, but hearing her voice removed from her body was somehow harder than not hearing from her. I was always waiting for her to call anyway – just like we were always waiting for snow to fall.

'I think he fancies you,' Crystal said then, as if she was fed up with the sorry lilt my consciousness. Her chin was no longer resting in her palm. She wasn't gazing over at Ace anymore. Her eyes were lilac and pouring into mine like lava made from Parma Voilets.

I had a sudden craving for Parma Voilets.

'Who?' I said. 'Who fancies me?'

'Ronald fucking McDonald,' Crystal said. We both laughed. I felt inconceivably happy.

'He was looking at your tits,' she said.

'He wasn't,' I said, unhappy again, confused about who she meant by *he* but more upset by her reference to breasts, 'because I don't have any.'

'No,' Crystal said, 'but soon you will.'

'No I fucking won't.'

She started to laugh, then seemed to realise I'd meant what I'd said. Through the smudged discolouration of her shades, I saw her see my knowledge of the Universe differently.

Or I thought I did.

'OK then, maybe you won't one day. Who knows? Maybe you'll be able to decide exactly how your body grows.'

She paused.

'Maybe eventually everybody will.'

Her jaw snuck into that grin of hers. I was on the brink of grinning again too, but then she said—

'Listen Daniela, I've never seen it, this second moon of yours.'

'It's not *mine*,' I snapped back, hating Crystal for saying my name, hating her, now, for everything. I was thirteen and though puberty was still properly to happen to me, already I hated the sound of it. I felt estranged from the word as much as I felt estranged from my own name, *puberty*, so fleshy and putrid; *Daniela*, so stupid and frilly. I was what was sometimes called a slow-starter and fine with that. My body still fit me but at the same time, I already sensed I didn't belong to it. I already sensed my body's future wasn't mine – not completely. Sat there in the grim brilliant light of the McDonald's, my own skinny ribs dug into me. I felt tears threatening. Crystal reached across the table as if to retrieve her sunglasses from where they'd slumped, lowslung, to the bump of my nose, but then she just pushed them back up for me.

'OK, kidda,' she said, half laughingly, half tenderly.

I didn't know where she'd got that word from, *kidda*, but I liked it. It was better than the name she'd just used for me.

'Let's make a deal,' Crystal said. 'You show me your second moon, and *I'll* prove to you I'm a murderer.'

'OK,' I said, tears fully fought. I bit into my fish burger and teased out the gherkin. Crystal plunged a finger into a broken sachet of ketchup, licked a little of it, then held her reddened tip out to me. She was waiting for me to taste what remained of the ketchup, I realised.

I didn't.

Then I did.

'Blood promise!' Crystal exclaimed. Her finger slipped between my shocked lips then shot back out again. Whatever was between us had now been consummated. Crystal fiddled with her hair nonchalantly. I shoved aside the remains of my fish burger. I wasn't hungry anymore. Then – as if she really could hear what I was thinking, as if she was psychic – she said—

'Don't worry about Mika. He's a hypocrite.'—

—'Why?' Fin asks, interrupting again, after a long period of silence.

'Why what?' Daniel sighs.

'Why do you think Crystal called Mika a hypocrite?'

'I don't know. I *didn't* know. And anyway,' Daniel continues, recollecting Fin's use of the word *version* when speaking of Crystal, 'How did you know about the existence of Crystal? It was you who first brought her up – it was you who first mentioned her name when you said that you thought I was like her. But how did you even *know* about her?'

'*Hypocrite*,' Fin says, thoughtfully, obliviously, 'is the Greek word for *actor*, but literally it means *an interpreter from underneath*.'

'OK,' says Daniel, by now becoming more accustomed to Fin's little obliquities, or maybe just more resigned to them. 'Thanks.'

'You're welcome.'

The sun blinks. The cruise ship lets out a little bleat – she sounds more like a newborn than a shipwreck. Daniel ponders the sound, then sighs again. 'It's such a queer feeling!' Daniel exclaims.

'What is?'

'The feeling of needing to tell you this story, without really knowing why it's necessary – without having a clue why.'

'But I think you do have something of a clue,' Fin says, grey eyes coolly glistening. 'It's a long time since you've thought about Crystal, isn't it?'

'Yes,' says Daniel, softly, relenting. The sleeve of Daniel's T-shirt is still stained with blood; Daniel's eyes are still a hot tone of amber. 'Yes, it is I guess.'—

—It's possible I've compressed these conversations. It's possible I told Crystal what I thought I knew about the Universe on a different day to the day she said she was a murderer, but on both occasions we were sat in the same booth in the same McDonald's in the same salt-mining lift-making diminuendo of a town, so maybe it doesn't matter. Maybe it didn't matter. It – what Crystal insisted she'd confessed to – didn't stop me from walking up the wide road with her the next morning and the morning after that, and it didn't stop me from watching her crush the ends of her *Luckys* and wanting to crush a cigarette just like her, and it definitely didn't stop me from wearing her sunglasses.

I wore them constantly, even inside, even while sleeping. I'd wake up in the night from my makeshift bed on the settee and fret for them, worried I'd broken them. Or else I'd wake with an arm poked into my cheek, denting it, artificially dimpling it. I took the sunglasses off when I went to school – when I actually went to school – because I knew I'd be teased for wearing them. Either that, or I thought somebody would have accused me of stealing them. Otherwise I kept them on all the time, wearing out the parts of the arms that hooped over my ears so that the plastic there faded.

I didn't care. Wearing Crystal's sunglasses helped with something, though I could never quite put my finger on what it was that was helped – what exactly it was that the sunglasses corrected, by distorting.

I watched T.V. through them, read *The Sun* through them, stood staring at my glum sorry body in my mum's long mirror through the finger-print-patterned lenses of them. Sometimes I tripped on a fissure that had ripped a zigzag through the road, because Crystal's shades disturbed the peripheries of my vision. Sometimes I thought I saw a freshly formed ditch in the ground, a brand new instance of subsidence tickling the curb or bullying somebody's front door, but then I'd think that I was just seeing things. I couldn't see clearly and not seeing clearly was simultaneously a relief and a difficulty.

I once watched Crystal semi-submerged in the bathtub through the sunglasses she herself had given me. I don't know whether she had wanted me to see her or whether the scene was intended for Mika, whether at that point Crystal was as intent on getting his attention as her oversized PJs were desperate to stay on her shoulders. I didn't know what she thought his attention would have given her, had she actually succeeded in getting it, but in any case she left the bathroom door ajar.

She'd gotten hold of a stereo from somewhere, a double cassette deck with no CD player. It wasn't mine but it might have been Mika's. She'd plugged it into the socket on the landing and trailed the cable through into the bathroom – she must have done that knowing it was dangerous. The bathroom light was on but the landing was dark. It must have been evening. Had I glanced through the small porthole window at the landing's end, I might have caught sight of the second moon, the moon Crystal said was *my* moon. The sunny sagas of *Home & Away* were all over again; or maybe it was just the ad break. The tape Crystal was playing was something by George Michael – of course it was. She was taunting Mika or trying to at least, because when I stared through her shades through the chink between the door and the doorframe, I could tell that she sensed somebody standing there, and that she was pleased by it – I could tell that she was trying to express something.

It was the only time I ever saw her hair messed. Her fringe was damp and uncrimped and sticking, like seaweed straggling on a rock, to her forehead. She cupped her hand over her stomach like she had done that first time in our kitchen, except now her belly was bare but for the suds of the foam and the bobbing silhouette of my mum's rubber ducky. I'd always thought my mum had loved that rubber ducky, but when she'd left, she'd not taken it with her. Crystal smothered the ducky's head with her palm, plunged the body of it under the water, watched it pop up again. Then she moved her hand slowly upwards, caressed the curves of her own breasts, and said – to who, I don't know; I didn't know, because already by then Crystal knew that I didn't want to grow tits, couldn't really believe I ever would do – 'You like them, don't you?'

I legged it. —

—'I've never,' says Daniel, 'told anybody this.' And then, hesitantly, 'No wonder it took me so long to figure out I liked girls – that I fancied women not men. Crystal really confused me.'

'I wouldn't have thought it would have taken you long,' Fin says, smiling that cute wry smile again, 'by the way you describe yourself when you were younger.'

The sky smarts, as if stung. The gull that Fin calls a pterosaur lets out a curdled cry; the cry thrums Daniel's eardrum – *Ow! What a sound!* – then everything goes quiet again.

I could start an argument, but I can't be bothered, thinks Daniel, annoyed by Fin's comment but deeply involved, now, in the

> story of Crystal's visit, even if its significance is still shifting and indeterminate, not fully understood, not yet, by Daniel:—

—In time my bedroom became hers. I went in sometimes when she wasn't there, ostensibly to fetch a fresh sweatless T-shirt. I'd run my fingertips over the cutting-collaged walls and try to tell if the smell of my duvet was different because of her. She caught me one time with my nose touched to the fabric. I remember sensing her presence before I saw her – she was stood there watching my bent body just like I'd watched her bare body buffered by bath suds. Her head was gently at rest against the doorframe, like an old gravestone leaning against a tree trunk. Not that there were many old gravestones where we lived – apart from some remnants of graveyards that had survived the town's planners, the cemeteries were the same age as the houses. There were still many vacancies. Mika said that everybody would be better off cremated anyway, and when I'd said that cremation wasn't always OK depending on somebody's religion, he'd turned his eyes to the stubborn skies, slapped his palms together and prayed for religion to die. It had taken me a while to realise he was joking.

Crystal's grey clouds rolled over me.

'What are you doing?'

'What do you think?'
'Sicko. Pervert.'
'I'm not a pervert.'
'No?'

I ripped the duvet off from the top of my bed, felt the flumpy material collapse in my hands.

'No. I'm doing the washing.'

It was always me who did the laundry anyway. I'd done it ever since my mum left. Or not quite *ever since* – when she'd gone the plastic latticed basket in the bathroom had filled up then overflown, but Mika had never so much as looked at it.

I bounced the duvet out of its cover the better to convince Crystal of my innocence. She wasn't supported by the doorframe anymore – her body was upright and her eyes, I realised, when mine were drawn to them by what she said next, were alert and frightened.

Or that's what I thought I saw – indoors, sunglasses made it hard to be sure.

'Don't touch my clothes. I'll take them to the laundrette or something.'

'It's alright. I don't mind.'

The laundrette was a decent walk away; the air outside its doors was always scolding and brash, as if the air there was so clean it could sting you.

'I said I'll take them the laundrette, OK?'

'OK,' I said.

The days went by and still no snow came, but the salt mine stayed open and Crystal kept staying with us. Mika must have been relieved about the mine and not having to scrabble about for alternative work, but he still relentlessly checked the forecast on Teletext while scratching his moustache, and he never relaxed into Crystal's presence in the house – if anything he just became colder. He sometimes behaved towards her as if she had caused him some unnameable injury, or no, as if she could do, should he lower his guard and allow her. It seemed to me that she gave up on him eventually, but it was difficult to tell, because Mika's moods grew complete and impassable. Or maybe that's not quite the right word – maybe I should say *impermeable* – but *impassable* is how his moods felt: they felt like invisible obstacle courses arranged across the ordinary world, sinkholes right there in there in the middle of the room, even to me, and I knew to expect them.

Crystal never joined us on the settee to watch T.V. – 'That sofa is gross and disgusting,' she had said to me, and then, unbelievably, in that same snapped tone she'd used the day she'd first arrived, 'I don't know *how* you can possibly sleep on it' – but sometimes on her way out of the house or back from somewhere she'd been without me, she would strut between the settee and the T.V. set, and I'd risk missing a key detail in *Neighbours* because of her body. I'd wish there was a way of immediately rewinding the episode, like with a VHS or like the way that one day, not so far into the future but still hardly imaginable then, it would be possible to do with T.V. – when T.V. became digital as opposed to analogue, I mean.

Then I'd wish that I'd never wished such a thing, because what if when I re-wound *Neighbours* I discovered something slightly amiss, something that hadn't happened in the version of the story that was continuing without me – some tiny but world-crushing detail?

Crystal said nothing more about murdering, about having killed somebody, about proving to me she was truly a murderer. I tried watching her for clues but had no clue what I was looking for; I was like a rookie detective who didn't know where to look. The way Mika was to her was hard to make sense of, and perhaps exactly for that reason I associated his shunning silences with the strangeness of her assertion, but at the same time that connection was flimsy and insubstantial. Everything in the world would just suddenly seem so flimsy and unsubstantiated – even the second moon I had recently been so sure of, even Mika's coldness to her. It was difficult to pin down, I mean, and though I could tell you about times like when he entered the kitchen in the evening and saw us both eating bowls of his favourite cereal, and he looked at Crystal as if *she* was a sicko, or even obscurely demeaning herself, and Crystal caught his look and slowly, surely regurgitated her mushed cereal into her cereal bowl – if I told you about that or any other wordless cruelty, what would I have told you?

The most you could say is that Crystal refused to hold the humiliation Mika attempted to give to her, which was more than I'd ever managed, and for that, though again I couldn't have said this back then, I admired her.

Like the snow didn't, we drifted. Maybe there never had been anything between us. Maybe nothing had been consummated by the ketchup I'd briefly tasted on her fingertip and I'd just wanted something from Crystal that Crystal couldn't have given me, which I think I'm now beginning to see was recognition of something I had no words for, but at the same time *only* words for, something caught up with the oncoming awkwardness of my body and in a funny way hers too, but which also had to do with what was I called, how the world heard me, how the world unheard me. How could Crystal have worked that conundrum out for me. She had her own stuff going on,

and as I would go on to do with people
I knew in the future, friends and lovers
and others too—

> —'Maybe,' Daniel says, looking at Fin both
> crossly and fondly, if that's possible, 'I'm
> even doing it with *you*.'—

—I mistook her shrill sadness and glittering dissatisfaction for an understanding of mine, for care, for tenderness.

Increasingly she'd be gone at odd times and get back late at night or early in the morning, her shoe straps hooked over her pinkies, her chiselled cheeks rosy with broken capillaries. I knew those to be caused by booze or abrupt changes in the weather – my mum had referred to them as *weather veins*, though the faces they flushed were usually older than Crystal's. Usually the faces they stained belonged to men skulking from pubs that also served as church halls or vice versa. Maybe Crystal was the karaoke version after all, I thought. Maybe I'd always be stuck in the karaoke version and Crystal was a golden ticket that had turned out to be fake, or what the ticket had promised was just disappointing. I told myself my feeling that she could hear what I was thinking without me outwardly communicating it was just superstitious, like believing that leaving shoes on the table was unlucky, or worse, fatal for somebody, though not necessarily the body who had left the shoes where they shouldn't have been.—

—'*Kleos*,' says Fin, 'was also the Greeks' word for *song*. It means both fame and the way the fame is communicated.'—

—I stopped bothering watching out for fresh depressions in the ground too, though soon my slackening would come to seem premature.

Crystal still sometimes mussed my hair semi-affectionately, and she still sometimes involved me in some of her cruel whims, like the time we were walking along the side of the wide road and saw an elderly woman whose polyethylene bags had popped on account of their load, and Crystal swung her arm across my midriff to stop me from helping. The bags' contents cascaded across the cracked pavement in front of us – tins and tins of baked beans and pineapple chunks, Hundreds and Thousands to sprinkle on ice cream, but no tub of ice cream. When the woman saw that we weren't going to help – when I saw her worn shrivelled face lift then fall again – I felt a flutter of delight before I felt guilty.

'Have a nice day!' Crystal yelled as we stepped over the detritus.

'We should have helped her.'

Crystal half-laughed like I'd said something ridiculous that wasn't worth properly laughing at. Then she smashed the stub of a *Lucky* into a brick wall, strode on in her heels ahead of me.

I never really thought about it much at the time, but it was curious, Crystal's endless supply of cartons of cigarettes. It was like they appeared in her pockets *ex nihilo*, from nowhere but constantly, neither bought from the shop nor flogged cut-price illicitly.—

—'So where,' Fin asks, though Daniel won't be able to answer, 'do you think she got them from?'—

—She never seemed worried about how many cigarettes she smoked or the possibility of running out, though she never, not after that first day in the kitchen, offered me another of her *Luckys* either.

Then there was the day we came across a kid trying to teach himself how to ride a bike without stabilisers. He was clumsy and struggling but perseverant, determined to accomplish the task he had set himself, and his keenness affronted Crystal. It was like she couldn't stand the sight of it.

She dragged me over to the crumpled strip of road where he was attempting, over and over again, to mount the seat of his bike and ride it successfully. In the near distance was the newsagents I sometimes stole sweet little nothings from, and beside it a betting shop. Mika had told me bookies were dungeons of hopefulness – he'd said they showed it was stupid to be hopeful. I tried to take my mind off the encounter that was about to happen by watching a bald man watch a screen inside. Crystal stood completely still by my side, the weight of her body supported by one dead straight leg, the other leg tilted at the knee and slightly hovering. Crystal often stood that way. It was a pose that was both knowing and noncommittal, readied but simultaneously disinterested. The boy saw us standing there but didn't say anything. I adjusted my oversized sunglasses. Then – she was improvising, I think, but there was also an intent to her maliciousness that made it seem purposeful – Crystal announced that I had some advice for him.

Her voice sounded like the sonic equivalent of a Sour Tongue, those sweets that are bitter and have two flavours.

'No I don't,' I huffed.

'Yes you do.'

'I *don't*.'

Crystal tutted at me then smiled kindly at the boy, whose tiny rattail I caught sight of just in time to be envious of.

'I'm Crystal. This is Daniela.'

I cringed at the frill at the end of my name – the 'a' I would soon drop silently, without telling anybody, like litter or like one of those bottle cap grips that sometimes got snagged on the roof of my mouth before I spat the barbed plastic hoop out into the trash and it wound its way, eventually, to a landfill.—

—'Or,' Fin adds, 'out to sea.'

'Yes,' says Daniel, and then, 'Though I guess it would depend on where the hoop was thrown away. I don't know. How *does* plastic ever end up in the sea?'

In the waves that swish below the cliff, plastic bags contract and relax, contract and relax. *The way they move through the water makes them look exactly like jellyfish*, thinks Daniel.

A beat passes.

'By the way,' Fin says, eyes skimming the sea's drossy surface, 'Did you notice how many moons were in the sky earlier? There are none now, but before there were two – here, I mean, where we are. Did you see them?'

Daniel, however, is still busy pondering the plastic bags. *Maybe they* are *jellyfish*, Daniel thinks, before continuing:—

—The boy was looking at me cautiously. *You're that girl who looks like a boy*, I thought he must have been thinking.

You're that kid who goes around wearing sunglasses all the time.

Crystal had meanwhile placed her hand on my shoulder. I could smell the smell I'd been searching for in the turquoise sea of my duvet.

'Daniela's *special*,' she said, with complete seriousness.

The boy blushed like I'd done when Crystal had called me *love*. It seemed like a long time since Crystal had called me that.

'You want an autograph?'

The boy squinted, unsure and intimidated.

'The trick is to keep your hands *off* the handlebars,' Crystal said, shoving my skinny ribs with her hip as she spoke, 'while keeping your eyes closed.'

The boy looked up at her then like she might have been his guardian angel. His eyes, like mine, were amber. For a moment I was surprised that he could be so gullible, so trusting.

Then I was disgusted.

'Joking!' Crystal exclaimed. The boy scowled, kicked a stray stone frustratedly. Crystal reacted ridiculously quickly, trapping the pebble beneath the chunk of her heel and leaning down to scoop it up.

I wanted to tell her to leave the boy alone, but I didn't.

'It's OK,' she said. 'It's to help him,' she said, and then, with a gesture much older than she was, she placed two fingers under his chin, lifted it, eased the grey spherical stone into his mouth.

He stared at her, kept the stone entombed. Crystal's body exploded. 'It's to ground you,' she said, silly with extreme laughter, 'It's to *stabilise* you.'

A moment later she was deadly serious again.

'Have you ever thought about what it would feel like to be abducted?' Crystal said to me, as we watched the boy push his bike up to speed then throw himself over the body of it, mounting it. The question alarmed me. Crystal must have been reading the cuttings on my bedroom wall closely, I thought. How else could she have known that abduction was something I'd sometimes wished for? I'd morbidly imagined it would have made everything easier, to disappear physically, as opposed to virtually.—

—'Virtually?' asks Fin.

'I guess I just mean metaphorically. I don't mean I disappeared into computers or video games, if that's what you're getting at.'

'Oh,' Fin says, inconclusively. 'OK.'

'The only game I remember playing at this age,' Daniel says, recollecting, elaborating, 'was LOGO on the computers at school, where you made little line drawings by telling a turtle what to do using simple programming commands.'

Where Fin and Daniel are, the sea churns. There are no turtles in its trashy waters, only jellyfish that might be plastic bags or vice versa, and polymer ornaments.

'LOGO doesn't sound like much of a game,' Fin says.

Daniel frowns, watches the gushing waves.

'No, but I guess the point of those early programmes was that they taught you *how* to be a programmer. They taught you how to build something new, using another language, as opposed to navigating a world that was ready-made.'—'

—'Actually, have you ever thought about how it would feel *to* abduct somebody?' Crystal asked next, and I got the funny feeling that she was shifting her query to shove me somewhere I wasn't sure I wanted to go, fine-tuning it, exactly calibrating it.

The boy rolled out of our sightline. We never saw whether he fell or not.

'Nothing *ever* happens here,' Crystal spat into the silence left my lack of response to her questions, and I felt sorry, then, that I had let her down. I expected her to curse me or our town or both, to mutter something like *it's so fucking tedious*, but instead she turned her anger upon herself – 'It's my fault. It's all my fault,' she said.

Her lilac-grey eyes were big and watery.

'What is?' I said, afraid of her sudden distress, unbearably aware of it like a *Neighbours* cliff-hanger. 'What's your fault, Crystal?'

But then – just like that – her body clammed up again. Just like that, her little scenes would come to seem arbitrary and unmotivated, and all I could feel was that we were drifting, that I was losing her even though there was nothing really to lose.—

—'Even though,' Fin says, 'you'd never really been close. Or had you?' —

—I still wore her sunglasses all the time. I still wanted to think the world of her. Whatever ambivalence I felt I transposed into jealousy; fists of jealousy kept forming in my belly, steadying me even while they unsteadied me, and as the weeks went by I comforted myself by convincing myself that something was going on between Crystal and Ace, something I was locked out of and barred from.

I say *comforted*, but the thought was tortuous.—

—'*Tortuous* means twisting or indirect,' Fin says. 'I think what you mean is *torturous*.' —

—On lukewarm Saturday afternoons that should have been colder, much colder, I'd hear a car pull up close to our house and holler its horn. Crystal would come downstairs from my room before I even heard the horn go. I'd watch her strut unhurriedly down the hall, her fringe freshly crimped, her lips liquid pink, her sweatshirt and gilet swapped for a puffer jacket and her shoes now huge chunky black boots. I never once saw Crystal dress for the weather. She wore clothes that always seemed to belong elsewhere—'

—'But then I guess I was also prone to that habit,' Daniel adds, in another voice, a lower voice, a voice that almost sounds like it might know something Daniel doesn't yet.

Where Fin and Daniel are, snow falls, falls, falls. Or it seems like snow – it looks exactly like snow – *but it's not snow, not really*, Daniel recalls Fin saying earlier. *Fin said maybe it's* me *who's snowing,* Daniel remembers, frowning, again vaguely disgruntled.

'It was like my fingers and toes were eternally dipped in Slush Puppie mixed from the melting glaciers,' Daniel says, 'while my head was stuck in the clouds that never let go over their load, the same clouds that kept disappointing Mika.'

'Slush Puppie?' asks Fin.

'Syrup mixed with piles of crushed ice,' replies Daniel. 'Don't you know it? It looked radioactive and chemically but tasted cool and delicious. But anyway, Crystal's clothes were something else.'—

'—and she always seemed to have more than I thought ought to be possible stuffed into her suitcase, the one with the white band with fluorescent green stripes tied to it. I'd investigated it once, during a sleuthing trip into my ex-bedroom. Tucked inside the netted partition were three incongruous volumes: a glossy holiday brochure and a battered hardback *Wham!* almanac and between them, *An Introduction to Feminism.* I hadn't known what to make of that strange trinity and my guilt about trespassing prevented me from ever questioning Crystal.

When she exited the house, called by the car's horn, I'd watch her figure deplete from the threshold, the toes of my Reeboks crunching the rough bristles of the doormat. I'd watch her figure deplete from the threshold of the house, the toes of my Reeboks crunching the rough bristles of the doormat. I never saw the car or Crystal in it – I just assumed she'd gone with Ace to the *flash*, which was a fake lake that had formed from subsidence, subsidence that had happened some time ago. Some of the companies that used the mined salt to make chemicals sometimes dumped their toxic waste in its waters. Men and their dogs ate sandwiches by its grim shores on Sundays. On Saturday nights it was where the teenagers of our town went to make out – the flash was like a rite of passage, though I'd never been there.

I never would, as it turned out. The flash disappeared the day of the massive collapses.—

—'The Great Subsidence?' Fin asks.

'Yes,' says Daniel, 'though there wasn't that much that was *great* about it, and in a way calling what happened by that name just seems absurd, because who's ever heard of the Great Subsidence? Nobody.'

Out at sea, the cruise ship tilts, then quickly rebalances. The movement, though almost indiscernible, spurns spasming ripples in the junky waves; cartons and bottles bob and lurch, bob and lurch, bob and lurch, though Daniel and Fin see only a blurry mass of them.

'Since then there's been so many huge disturbances,' Daniel says, 'disasters that everybody's heard of. The fires, the floods, the accelerating erosions. The Great Subsidence was but a brief wrinkle on the surface of the world, and but a tiny one.'

'That's true,' says Fin, 'but I think that's also the point.'

'What do you mean?' asks Daniel.

Cartons and bottles bob and lurch, bob and lurch. Plastic bags-cum-jellyfish contract and relax.

'Just that scale is deceptive,' Fin says dazedly, staring out to sea. Fin's long eyelashes are collecting a pillowing of snowflakes; Fin's curtains are no longer perfect. 'If you think about it, everyday objects are also disasters, miniature catastrophes. The little things that make it possible to get through the day, like your toothbrush, or those bottle cap grips that sometimes got stuck in the roof your mouth – by which I think you mean the tamper seal, the breakaway band that's supposed to stay put when you unscrew the cap and lift the bottle up to your lips. Have you ever thought about how those are manufactured? Where they're produced and by whom? How many hours of a life the making of them consumes?'

On the snowy cliff edge, Daniel shifts about moodily.

'I have actually,' Daniel says, truthfully, and also a little petulantly. 'I told you I wondered about Mika's cigarette papers, didn't I?'

'Everybody always tends to assume,' Fin says, ignoring Daniel's answer, 'that objects become sad when they turn into trash, when they accumulate out of context in a state of disuse, or as pollution. But objects are already sad before that

– so many objects are little microcosms of melancholy, of labour painstakingly done then quickly forgotten, days and days rendered invisible, or just as disposable as the objects they're spent making go on to be.'

In the funny sky above the sea, the gull-like creature lets out another scream. The sun is still red and piercing.

The ripples in the sea diminish and allay.

'I guess so,' Daniel says, struck by Fin's thoughtfulness but somehow unsurprised by it, before continuing again:—

—We never spoke of Mika's silences or Crystal's plans for the future and by this point our ritual trips to McDonald's had dwindled.

Some days Crystal claimed to be watching her weight – I said nothing of her habit of sucking McNuggets, not eating them – some days she slept late, very late, and some days she said she had somewhere she had to be for something that was important. When she said that she winked with the eye that once had been bruised – her poorly eye healed eventually, of course it did – and I wasn't sure if she was serious. Once she returned wearing a pair of earrings that dripped down from her earlobes, with turquoise stones of diminishing size, and on the backside

of one I saw a tiny line engraving – a little
coffin that dangled right next to the place
on her neck where her pulse would have
pulsed, had I felt for it.—

> —'Like this?' Fin asks, holding out a wrist.
> 'Yes,' Daniel replies, staring at Fin's tiny
> tattoo, only now recognising its resemblance to the engraving on Crystal's earrings. 'Exactly like that.'—

—Ace must have given Crystal the earrings, I thought. I didn't think she could
have had the money for them. She'd told
me she was working shifts in a pub named
for a racehorse but there was no regularity to her coming and goings, and though
I'd once caught her scouring the crummy
crevices of our settee cushions, I didn't
think she'd have dared taken money
directly from Mika's wallet. I had a paper-round that involved packing newspapers
with flyers and sample sachets of luminous detergent – that was how I knew
about the process of sodium and chloride, by the way, from scanning the listed
ingredients repeatedly – but more often
than not I shoved stacks of folded papers
and their bloated interiors into wheelie
bins, and Crystal had never helped me
with it. I doubted her dead mum could
have left her much – though it was possible the earrings had previously been her

mum's, and Crystal had just started wearing them.

But when I asked her where the earrings had come from, she just grinned and said, 'What does it matter, kidda?' she grinned, when I asked her where the earrings had come from, and when I held my nerve and kept her for an answer, she tossed her grey eyes, which turned lilac as they rolled, shook her head so that her crimped fringe shivered, said 'Nobody. Nowhere. OK?'

I missed her.

I missed her even though she was still there – not properly *gone*, like my mum or her mum.

When Crystal went off with Ace, or when I assumed she'd gone off with him, I sank into the settee beside Mika feeling desperate without knowing what I was desperate about: whether I wanted Crystal all to myself, or whether I wanted what Crystal seemed to be – not a *little girl*, but not a woman either – or whether I wanted to give Crystal whatever I fuzzily imagined *she* wanted, what she was looking for, which wasn't something I knew or was in any way sure of. All I was sure of was her changeable temperament and surging, lunging frustration – her way of saying things that seemed significant one minute, flippant and meaningless the next, her way of making me feel caught and thrown simultaneously. Or maybe it was Ace I was envious of – maybe it was somebody like him that I wanted to become, the kind of boy Crystal would want to hang out with. Confronting the thought that I never would – not unless something entered my world that wasn't already there, something wild and crazy impossible – made *me* feel both murdered and murderous, which in turn returned me to the question of what Crystal had meant when she'd said she would prove she was a murderer.

Was this Crystal's proof? The way she was making me feel inside?

At least I had her sunglasses to hide my saddening eyes.

Eventually something happened that in retrospect seems like a turning point, though at the time it hardly felt that way.—

> —'That's the thing about stories,' says Fin, annoyingly, *but not*, Daniel will think, when Fin finishes speaking, *without a point*. 'They turn what seemed impossible at the time into what was necessary.'—

—One morning when I should have been in school but wasn't, I saw Ace without seeing Crystal. Crystal wasn't with him, I mean, which surprised me, because by then I was accustomed to thinking that Crystal was with Ace whenever I didn't know where she was or might have been. I'd never been up to McDonald's without her. I'd never felt like Filet O' Fish for breakfast unless breakfast was spent with Crystal. The morning I saw Ace I was sat in a bus shelter – not the shelter with the liverspotted roof visible from my bedroom window, but another one deeper into town, on the edge of the grey angular shopping centre that few people now used on account of the cheaper stores and cheaper goods in the retail parks on the town's circumference. The shelter stood opposite a playground. It was a good playground – good intentioned. The climbing frame and its covered slide looked like a miniature replica of the overground buildings belonging to the salt mine. The paint on the structures was patchy and mottled, overcome with an overgrowth of mossiness. The playground was the haunt of truants like myself – *skiving*, we called it – some of whom were high as kites they never flew by nine in the morning, some of whom came to the playground to push pretty much everything but the soggy seat of a swing, long before they should have heard of their product range.

I felt drawn to that playground like I felt drawn to the headline on my bedroom wall – *I DECIDED TO GET HIGH, BUT I WOULD NOT SAY I HAD A CHOICE.*

Though I was still barely thirteen, I'd gotten high a number of times before Crystal came to stay with us. Since she'd arrived I hadn't. I wasn't high the time I saw Ace, but I was probably looking for the opportunity to be. I already wanted to try more than I'd tried, which was just weed and half a dab of acid, which came on a tiny torn piece of blotting paper, which you took on your tongue like the melting body of a god and then waited for the world to melt likewise. I couldn't have said why I wanted, so much, to get high – I'd just felt the need to ever since I'd understood it was possible, as if my getting high was inevitable or necessary like fate, and therefore better to get going with, to get over and done with. Crystal's visit had distracted me from a lot of stuff that bothered me – the feeling of needing to get high tagged along with me like a shadow, not mine just obstinately attached to me – but without her by my side I was again solitary and mooching and bored, and school was school was school. It was still some imitation of winter. My bum was resting on the bus shelter's tilted seat as I observed the shapes made by the playground in its near emptiness.

Ace came round the corner, walked past me, stopped, came back again.

'Hi kidda.'

Kidda was Crystal's word for me.

'Hi.'

He was wearing a tracksuit with one leg rolled up. His hair was perfectly curtained, like always.

'Nice sunglasses.'

I didn't say anything. Ace had seen me wearing Crystal's sunglasses before, without feeling the need to comment on them.

'Where's your sister?'

The question confused me. Why didn't Ace know where Crystal was? Nothing made sense if Ace didn't know.

'She's not my sister,' I said, instead of asking Ace where she was.

'No?'

'Nope.'

'You ever go to school?'

'Why aren't *you* at work?'

Ace grinned a flashy grin at me. His grin was too toothy for his good looks, but I liked him more for it. My own teeth were similarly crooked – fanged at the front and disrupted. Ace came and sat on the seat beside me and for a while we both stared straight ahead, watching a single kid spin solemnly round on the playground's merry-go-round. The kid wasn't playing. He was too big to be spinning for pleasure. His limbs were too gangly. His jaw was chomping on bubble gum as he spun – then he spat the gum out of his mouth, but because of the force of the merry-go-round going round, the gum got caught on the chest of his T-shirt.

The sky groaned.

I kicked a pop can from out under my feet. As I kicked it I thought I felt the ground subtly shift, then I thought I was probably imagining it. Knowing that subsidence was always a possibility made me half-expect the ground to cave constantly.

'I'm done working at McDonald's,' Ace said. 'I'm done with this sinkhole.'

Crystal would have said *shit* hole.

Ace told me he was going to university soon. He didn't say where or what he was studying. Then he started humming the *Home & Away* theme tune. The notes were off but I recognised it instantly – that song was always in my head too.

The kid on the merry-go-round fell off the merry-go-round.

Ace stopped humming. Then he said—

'I came here to look for my brother.'

The can I'd kicked rolled quickly, too quickly, across the unsloping pavement, slicked itself in a puddle that might have been piss, belly-flopped into the rut of the gutter.

'He comes here too,' Ace continued. 'Thinks he's clever for flunking school. He isn't.'

I didn't need a lecture.

'I'm not lecturing you. I'm not bothered what you do. I like your sunglasses. They're cute. I like how you wear them whatever the weather.'

'Yeah?'

'Yeah. Why do you think I let you have all those free brekkas?'

I'd thought the free fries and Styrofoam clamshells were for Crystal's benefit.

'It's my brother I'm looking out for,' Ace said, shaking his head, gently bashing his bangs together. His chin was lightly sprinkled with stubble. I touched the non-existent fuzz on my upper lip.

'Yeah?'

'Yeah. He'll kill all his chances if he's not careful.'

The kid in the playground re-mounted the merry-go-round. For a moment I thought it might have been the same boy Crystal and I had seen teaching himself to ride his bike without stabilizers, but when I saw the back of his head, I could tell that it wasn't. This kid didn't have that neat little rattail I'd been briefly envious of.

When I looked back at Ace, Ace was looking dead at me. '*You'll* always have a choice.'

I thought again of the headline from *The Sun*, the one cellotaped to my bedroom wall and the one that had caught Crystal's attention too, the one she had attempted to explain her badly bruised eye by. I DECIDED TO LIE, BUT I WOULD NOT SAY I HAD A CHOICE. I DECIDED TO DIE, BUT I WOULD NOT SAY I HAD A CHOICE. I DECIDED….ETC. ETC.

'Why?'

Ace stood up and re-rolled his trouser leg, tending it carefully. Then he walked forwards and stood facing towards the playground, toes touching the curb where the curb relinquished itself.

Then he swung abruptly back round again.

'Cos you're *white*, kidda. Haven't you noticed?'

He raised his eyes up to the sky, heavy but unyielding. I thought of Mika and the mine and the never-coming snow. I thought of Mika and the salt stuck to his eyelashes. I saw my own self-absorption and felt embarrassed. It seemed to me that Ace was going to walk away then, but he didn't. He stayed very still for a second.

Then he said—

'Your sister – or, OK, whoever she is – is nuts by the way. She likes to play games huh?'

Did he mean something sexual or did he mean he and Crystal played games together or had Crystal told Ace the same thing that she had told me, meaning he knew she was a murderer or might have been? I was tired of the murder mystery already. I was tired of missing Crystal even though she hadn't gone anywhere – I was tired of everything and nothing and anything.

Ace was looking straight at me again.

'She's full of shit, but there's something weird about the stuff that she says. It's like she's telling the truth even when you know she isn't. She makes you *feel* like she is, I mean. It's fucked up!'

His Adam's Apple bounced uncomfortably in his throat. He seemed, I thought, annoyed now.

'She should be a magician or something,' he said bitterly, as if it were an insult. 'She's a good manipulator.'

Ace shook his head at me and sighed with a hissing sound.

'Who hurt her?'

The question came from nowhere but felt like a memory. Ace's eyes were still intently on me and this time I felt like I understood exactly what he was asking, what it was that was meant by the question. I knew Ace wasn't asking about the origins of Crystal's bruised eye – since it had healed I'd almost forgotten it – but something else, something that would have explained her brittleness and riddles, her *Luckys* and cruelty, the broken mirror of Mika's, her bursts of kindness and skittish, unreliable attention.

There was nothing else like it, Crystal's attention, when it actually came for you. Lava made from Parma Violets.

'Her mum died,' I shrugged.

'I don't mean that,' Ace snapped. He seemed a strange kind of sad now, as if he was sad and angry simultaneously.

'She thinks *she's* winning, when really she's just self-destructing. I don't know, kidda. Do you reckon she believes her own stories?'

I said nothing. What Ace had said made me think again of Crystal's turquoise-jewelled earrings and her insistence on taking her own clothes to the laundrette, but at the same time, what Ace said explained nothing. I didn't have the answer to his question and neither, I thought – I mean the thought came to me then – would Crystal have done.—

—'Maybe not, but I think you were right to take Crystal seriously, or at least, to be willing to do so.' Daniel looks sharply at Fin, who carries on talking regardless. 'Maybe she was just trying to figure something out – like you're doing now.'

The sun shivers behind a flimsy cloud. The cruise ship tilts again, bleats again.

'So you keep suggesting,' Daniel replies, distractedly, confused by the whims of the sea-view, 'but I don't see how. I'll never know the truth or if Crystal's so-called confession meant anything, because what Ace said next—'

'Trust me,' Fin says before Daniel can finish, and then, when Daniel looks unconvinced, Fin shrugs and adds, 'Or just pretend to, if that makes it easier. It all ends the same way anyway.'

'*What* does?' Daniel asks, frustrated by Fin's claims and cryptic suggestions but entranced, too, by the sight of the cruise ship, which *definitely looks*, Daniel thinks, *less wrecked, less dilapidated than she did earlier.* 'What ends the same way anyway?

But Fin, however, doesn't answer.

The sun emerges from the flimsy cloud – or the cloud gives up on hiding it.

'It's so hard to tell a story well when you're not sure where it's going,' Daniel says, sadly, faintly.

'But part of you knows,' Fin replies, and then, when Daniel's face scrunches, 'OK, think of it this way. You already *are* where your story goes – you're sat on this cliff edge waiting for your story to catch up with you: to arrive here, to join you.'—

—'Anyway,' Ace said, already turning to go, 'I helped Crystal dump your old settee.'

'What?'

'I said I helped her get rid of your old sofa,' he repeated, yelling disaster casually over his shoulder, his body already orientated elsewhere. 'You're welcome!'

I watched, head-locked by shock, as Ace walked away. I didn't see where he went or whether he found his kid brother, because soon enough the shock turned to panic, and my body was hurtling ahead of me, my sunglasses wonky, my lungs burning from the movements my legs were doing without me doing anything, my skinny ribs clenched. I ran as fast as I could back to our pebbledashed house by the side of the wide road, because now it was Mika I was worried about killing somebody.

Or if he hadn't killed her, I was sure he'd have kicked her out – meaning Crystal would be *gone* too, and I would never have said goodbye to her.

Though saying so out loud still feels silly and nonsensical – *soft*, the boys in my school would have called it – I guess it must have been around this time that the feeling I should have been famous began to move in me. Should have been famous—

—'Recognised, known, loved, heard of,' Fin nods.—

—but never would be. That latter bit, that anticipatory let-down, was crucial. The feeling shifted in me like a tectonic instability; I don't think I necessarily felt it consciously and I don't know exactly where it came from, whether it had something to do with Mika's full name being *George Michael* or whether it was my version of the story of the blind woman from *The Sun* or whether it was just somewhere to send the unbearable unsustainable sense that something was somehow escaping me, stealing away from me, something to do with my true form and the hard contours of my body, which if Crystal was right and I would grow breasts, soon wouldn't be my body. Softly softly, the snow would not fall. I don't know, I didn't know. Maybe at the end of the day it was just another way of wishing myself away, of disappearing, or manufacturing my disappearance.

Unless it was the result of wearing of Crystal's sunglasses all the time – unless Crystal was to blame for everything.

When I made it back to our house from the bus shelter opposite the playground, Mika was sat in a deckchair in the space where the settee had once been, watching T.V. His eyes swung to mine then back to the screen, and his legs, which had been crossed when I crashed into the room, uncrossed themselves. By the deckchair, neatly folded by somebody, was the bedding that I had been using at night. I went over to it, shovelled my bum into its comforting cosiness, and watched whatever Mika was watching.

'Night,' he said later, when he went to bed.

'Night,' I said, and then I swapped the bedding for the brief warmth Mika had left in the depression of the deckchair, and waited for Crystal to come home.

These were still the years of landlines and payphones, and there was no way of knowing where somebody was when they weren't there, how long they would be, or whether they'd ever return.

Unsleeping, cheeks twinkling from the jittering glow of the T.V., still wearing my sunglasses, forever wearing those naff snazzy hand-me-downs, I sat in that deckchair waiting for Crystal and thought back to the weeks immediately after my mum had left. During that time, Mika had paved over the soil in our front yard. I'd watched him work from my bedroom window, my fingers gripping the sill that Crystal now put out her *Luckys* on. It must have been during one of the periods when the mine was closed on account of the unforthcoming snow, because Mika had worked all day and into the evening, first ripping the flowers up from the beds then dumping the severed heads by the side of the road, letting them wilt there. He'd mapped out the space of the patio – he had been adamant about calling it a *patio*, even though the area it covered encompassed the entirety of our yard, so that its surface area was undifferentiated from what once had been gravelly earth – with twigs and linked string, not unlike the plots by McDonald's. Then he'd collected the paving stones. He'd delivered them in shifts in an ancient cracked wheelbarrow, tipping out each load in an unsteady pile, making it difficult, almost impossible, to exit our house via the front door. It *was* impossible, for a half a day or so, and while I'd watched Mika work the thought had crossed my mind—

—'Funny, isn't it,' Fin says, not as a question, 'the thought of a thought crossing a mind, like a cloud crosses the sky.'—

—that that was what Mika wanted. He wanted to give somebody else the feeling of being confined underground, of being buried alive.

That was how Mika's moods had made me feel anyway, in the years after my mum left. Though I knew he must have been sad and mad about her going, somehow her departure wasn't the cause of them; I could never figure out what suddenly compelled him to stop speaking, whether it was my fault, whether I had done something to make him fade away. But at the same time, he never faded away. In that pebbledashed house by the side of the wide road, Mika's silences were inescapable. They made me endlessly search for a specific cause, even if there was only a general one – that was what was so painful about them. Later, much later, when the world was no longer analogue, when the world was webbed and searchable via the Internet, I came across a monochrome photograph of a row of miners' houses in a different town, not ours but somewhere where the mine was a coal mine, and each of the terraced houses were blank and without windows. Where the windows would have been, were bricks. They had probably been built that way to keep out the constant coal dust. I saw the photograph and thought of Mika's patio – I mean I saw the photograph and, like Ace's question about who had hurt Crystal, it felt like a memory of something but also a memory of nothing.

Or like a metaphor for something that the world no longer had any memory of.

As Mika had worked on the patio he'd worn thick gardening gloves. They'd made his hands look huge and cartoonish – they looked more like my mittens than gardening gloves, more like the hands of Ronald McDonald than his hands. Sometimes he would stop, pull the gloves off, and survey his progress. In his jean pockets he kept stashed miniature bottles of vodka, and when he stopped he would take a sip from one, his figure stark against the tarmac behind him, the horizon slicing a line through his torso. Then he'd wipe the sweat from his forehead with the sleeve of his T-shirt and sometimes I saw him lick the length of a bicep – he was licking for salt, I thought, for the sharp tangy taste of it. His sweat was forever thick with it, and when the sweat evaporated tiny crystals smeared his skin, making it seem like a slug had crawled up his neck and back down again between the breadth of his shoulders.

Except slugs were murdered by salt. I'd learnt that from my mum, who'd used salt to kill the slugs that made it to our porch from the soil in the yard that Mika paved over when she left.

I remember Crystal once telling me a story she'd heard somewhere, about a mum poisoning her own kid, a toddler. Over the course of maybe a year or more, the mum had gradually fed the kid toxic quantities of table salt. It was the only time Crystal ever really acknowleged the nature of her whereabouts while she was staying with us, the only time she seemed aware of our means of subsistence, our sustenance, though even then the reference was indirect and ambivalent. Crystal would have said it was just a coincidence. The story itself was set in Miami. 'You'd fit right in there, kidda,' I remember her saying to me, her lips splitting into a fleeting grin, her teeth denting the skin of the bottom one.

Crystal didn't know what the mum or the kid had been called, or how exactly they'd eventually caught her – how the police had realised it was her, the mother, who had been harming him.

'She got away with it for ages because nobody ever expected it of her,' Crystal said, her eyes distant but coolly glistening.

'Nobody could get their heads around the fact that a woman would do something like that to her own child, so nobody suspected her. Then when they accepted it was definitely her, they claimed that having the kid must have sent her crazy.'

She paused, sniffed, brushed her bright painted nails across the sore reddened caves of her nostrils.

'Nobody ever considered she might have had the kid just to live out her craziness. *In order* to torture it.'

And then—

'No wonder you don't want to be a woman, kidda!'

As far as I recall this wasn't a story I had cellotaped to my wall.—

—'It's only now,' Daniel adds, 'that I'm remembering this.'—

—In the evenings after finishing work on the patio, Mika had sat on the settee watching, what else, the T.V., his head heavy with the day's exertion and the vodka he'd drunk, plus the vodka he was drinking, plus the vodka he was still to drink. After my mum left I'd started making Mika his drinks for him, sometimes neat, sometimes mixed with sloppy splashes of Pepsi. I'd take the drink into him and balance it on the arm of the settee, where the fabric was worn and the padding would give a little. During the time that he had been busy constructing it, I'd never asked Mika why he was building the patio. How would I have done? I'd have had no idea how to formulate the question or still my fizzing fear of his frown and the likelihood that he'd have hated me for asking, so after a while I'd just stopped thinking about it.

But that night in the deckchair in front of the T.V., I thought about it.

He'd wanted something to be the same whatever the weather was, I thought. He'd wanted something to remain unchangeable. He didn't want our yard to be subject to the cruel whim of the seasons, to the way we were always waiting for snow or the way when it came, it came teasingly, and never enough to necessitate the great heaps of salt grit that would have kept the mine functioning year-round. He wanted some small part of his world to be unreachable by the conditions that otherwise formed it, I thought, and even while I understood that this was my fantasy, that it was possible I was imagining more in his mind than there necessarily was – even though it was possible he'd just been building a patio – I also understood, not *at* the time so much as *under* it, in a way I'm only really realising now, as I speak this, how my ideas about what was happening inside Mika masked something much more difficult to situate in relationship to reality, like the second moon or the treacherous ground of our town or the feeling I should have been famous but would not be.

My fantasies of Mika's motivations for building his patio masked a fantasy that Mika was dead inside, empty.

Less safe, and less tolerable, was the knowledge that Mika's internal world was as volatile and unpredictable as anybody's.

Even though it had been her who had left, even though it had been her who'd abandoned me, I'd always thought of my mum as the innocent party in the break-up. She hadn't been having an affair. Not as far as I knew. She hadn't left Mika for somebody or gone off to live with anybody, but she had obviously wanted the possibility of doing so. She had wanted the possibility of living a different life to the life she'd ended up living, and unless she left she'd never have known what she might have had instead – and unlike Mika, she'd been willing to risk that bigger disappointment. That was how it had it seemed to me. That was how I'd forgiven her, or how I thought I'd forgiven her. I never imagined – it never really occurred to me – that my mum had left because Mika was already ahead of her, already elsewhere as he sat sulkily thumbing *The Sun*, eating handfuls of nuts, batting his salt-crusted eyelashes.

'Can you see *anything* in those sunglasses?' Crystal said and said to me.

Your sunglasses, I always thought, whenever she said that, though I never corrected her. I never—

—But then instead of continuing, Daniel sighs deeply.

'What's wrong?' Fin asks.

'It's just so difficult,' Daniel replies. 'Just when I think I'm getting closer to the end, everything I say creates more to explain. I still don't know why I've felt the need to bring it all up again – just because *you* told me to tell a story.'

Daniel slumps back on the snow-topped ground, belly skywards.

'And I'm so tired. I can't remember when I last slept or when I last ate. I still have no real memory of how I ended up here – or where *here* even is for that matter.'

'It'll come to you,' Fin repeats, which tickles Daniel tired irritation. Daniel sits abruptly back up, scrunches a handful of snow in a fist, thinks of attempting to chuck it at Fin, but then, remembering what happened last time, thinks better of it.

'Hang on,' Fin says, getting up and walking a little away, away from the cliff edge. A few moments later, Fin returns, clutching two chilled cans of Pepsi.

'Wow,' says Daniel, gratefully taking a cold can. 'Thanks.'

'You're welcome,' Fin replies, with no explanation as to why the cans were left where they were.

Daniel sips, then squints. What earlier Daniel took to be a gull is now frolicking in the flumpy clouds; its long feathered body twists and turns. Then it hovers. Then it dips and soars. Head tilted, Daniel watches it. *It's definitely too big to be a gull*, Daniel thinks, perplexed but too weary to question Fin.

Fin takes a sip of Pepsi.

Daniel stifles a rising hiccup.

'When are you going to say more about changing your name?' Fin asks, tracing the airborne creature's line of flight with a finger, as if its line of flight were an autograph, but one that could never be repeated.

'I didn't change it,' Daniel replies, surprised by Fin's attention to detail, but also delighted. 'I just lost the last *a*, and anyway, it's only you who calls me Daniel.'

'Oh but *I've* never called you anything,' Fin says. —

—What happened next is hard to describe, and likely difficult to believe.

I must have fallen asleep in the deckchair at some point, because I didn't hear Mika leave for work, and though when I woke I had the funny feeling it had finally snowed, when I looked out the window I could see that it hadn't, so I must have been dreaming. There was no sign in the house of Crystal. I got up, got changed, left my sunglasses resting on the kitchen table, and went to school. The lessons were long and tedious, and in the break somebody teased me for stinking of B.O. I didn't care. Soon enough they sent us all home anyway, because they said there had been an accident.

Something had gone wrong underground in the mine, everybody was saying, and the ground had caved.

It was the start of the Great Subsidence. There had always been subsidence of some kind, Mika had warned me, but now the ground was everywhere treacherous. Curbs fell forever away from themselves, and structures were irrevocably tilted. Our house was among those that listed that very morning – I came across it abruptly, almost unexpectedly, having made my way back along streets and alleyways that no longer looked completely like their old selves, streets and passages that hadn't necessarily changed much – though some had – but which still seemed retouched because of what had happened, what was happening. Lopsidedly, our house leaned into the disturbed earth and it made it seem so ridiculously fragile, the way Mika's patio had erupted, avalanching soil and re-opening our front yard like a torn scab, or like a burial site without any bodies.

I was stood dazedly staring at the topsy-turvy when I sensed Crystal standing beside me.

'Wow,' she said. Her eyes were lilac without a hint of grey in them. She had her denim gilet on again. The collar had flopped down and between the blue denim and her turquoise-jewelled earring, I caught sight of something I knew, without doubt, was a love-bite.

'It's your fault!' I screamed at her. 'It's *all* your fault!' and then, stupidly, full of unnameable rage, 'You never should have moved the settee!'

She looked at me curiously for a moment, then shrugged, said she was freezing, removed her shoes and toed her way across the uprooted paving stones.

Her movements seemed to me to be supple and accomplished, the opposite of clumsy.

It's complicated. It's not that I thought Crystal had really caused what had happened, and it's not that I thought I'd solved her murder mystery, Crystal's strange interminable murder mystery. That's still going on, still continuing—

> —'Otherwise you wouldn't be here,' Fin nods. —

—still troubling me after all these years, even though I thought I'd forgotten it, or maybe because I did. It's more that when the floor finally went from beneath my feet - when the ground collapsed massively, improbably, tracing new cracks across town and obscuring routes home, turning bodies back and around and forcing about-turns – then, when the ground went, I saw what Crystal had set in motion when she'd said that she was a murderer and that she could prove it.

She'd made me look for her proof everywhere, in everything she said and did, to the extent that all I saw was what she wanted me to see—

> —'Or maybe I'm only seeing this now, not then,' Daniel says in another voice, that other, lower voice.
>
> Out at sea, the cruise ship's sides shine in the sun, which now is gradually lowering. *She looks less battered than she did before, I'm sure*, Daniel thinks.
>
> The sun, sinking a little, blinks again.
>
> The airborne creature Daniel thought was a gull turns a somersault, slips out of view again.
>
> 'Maybe it's only by telling this broken story to you,' Daniel says, still in that other voice, 'that I've come closer to understanding what Crystal was trying to communicate.'—

—which was just what she *wanted* to be capable of. Crystal wanted me to believe she was capable of killing somebody – that she had it within her, that she could have done it, given the opportunity. She wanted me to see that's all gender really is, what everybody expects of you on account of your body, your contours, but that at the same time, that's everything. That's nothing and that's all there is. She saw that and it made her angry – murderous. But just like the secretiveness I sensed in her when she first arrived at our house, her murderousness also belonged to me – like a memory of something I couldn't yet speak of, the 'a' I would soon drop from the end of my name, but silently, without telling anybody. There it went that very day, tumbling into the going ground.

Or at least, it makes sense to me now, sat here on this cliff edge, to say that that's how it happened.

I never did show Crystal the second moon. How could I have done? She left almost as suddenly as she'd turned up on our doorstep. She waited until we knew Mika was OK – he was caught up in the incident and injured – and then she went. I remember her packing that second-hand suitcase of hers, and that was the last time I saw her.

The salt mine closed immediately after the collapses, and then later indefinitely, creating a ghost town, or the ghost of a ghost town. Many moved away, though others remained – me and Mika amongst them, till I too left eventually. What once wasn't much turned to rubble and rubbishy nothingness. There wasn't enough work to go round at the elevator factory and there were only so many lorry jobs available and it would be ages, epochs, too late – for Mika's beat-up body anyway – till somebody would come up with the idea to bolster what was left of the mine's ruptured cavities and turn the underground rooms into storage, into archives.

The company who owned the mine claimed the structures were unsalvageable, beyond repair, and at the time Mika seemed soothed by that. He was given a payoff, which was something but not much, because they never resolved the inquiry into what actually happened that day, how the subsidence spread so massively, suddenly, devastatingly. Some thought the rockpit had been flooded by an underground reservoir of fresh water, others by a brine run that had been silently trickling for centuries, an overlooked remnant of the gone evaporated sea, though some claimed everything would have been OK, were it not for the workers. Somebody must have made an error, they said. Somebody must have gotten distracted. The inquiry went on and on until it was no longer running, and nobody cared, because everybody knew the collapses had long been a likelihood anyway. Everybody knew responsibility had always been frayed, ripped and raggedy and impossible to say if the collapses happened on account of malpractice or increased casualness and the pressure of corner cutting or just because the ground where we lived was worn out and sagging and ready for it all to be over and done with anyway, like the face of the woman whose plastic bags popped on her way her home from the shops, the woman Crystal stopped me from helping.

The woman I might never have helped anyway.

Though it would happen in his lifetime, I never knew what Mika thought about the mine's reclamation – about its transformation into the archives many years later. By then I'd left home and moved far away from the North, and by then I never bothered phoning him. He had less and less to say. The weather kept worsening and worsening, was sunny when it should have been overcast and vice versa, but I was doing OK and not succumbing. I leant on substances that kept me sane by keeping me out of it. Everybody still called me Daniela but ever since the Great Subsidence my name had been Daniel, and after hating cats for most of my life, I got two, and thought I saw the world die in their eyes – but the world had already died in the blanks of Crystal's sunglasses.

I must have first read about the mine's repurposing on the Internet.—

> —'By then,' adds Daniel, 'the Internet was everywhere, or at least increasingly ordinary, whereas when I was younger it had seemed fantastical. I remember first hearing about the existence of the World Wide Web – it must have been around the time of Crystal's visit – and not being able to *imagine* it.'—

—They had cleared out the rubble and installed shelves like great library stacks, and then they started keeping secrets down there: precious stones and floppy disks, records and memories, machines to read the floppy disks – machines to read software that might become extinct, or already had done; Amstrads and Megadrives alongside black and white photographs whose digital shadows had been uploaded online as well as hard copies of all the information people were worried would be irretrievably lost were the seasons to become completely unreasonable and the world become unwebbed again, were the world to experience another solar storm like the one that had happened over a century ago, when a solar coronal mass ejection spat out the sun's plasma and the spat plasma smashed into the planet, disrupting telegraph systems and causing dazzling auroras, fantastic showers of streaming multicoloured light. I knew all about that cosmic event as a kid. I probably should have mentioned it earlier – it was part of my knowledge of the Universe. I sometimes thought it could have been the cause of the split between our world and that other world, the world exactly like our own but with no knowledge of ours and just one solo moon, so when I learnt that the salt mine was being repurposed as archives, it seemed – I – I don't know—

—'I'm trying to say too much at once,' Daniel says, stumbling, stalling. 'I'm making a mess of it.'

Snow falls.

'You're doing fine,' Fin replies, and then, quietly, thoughtfully, 'The Great Subsidence makes me think of so many towns that disappeared, like the lost coastal city of Dunwich, which sank on account of repeated storm surges, or Craco in Italy where overexpansion caused landslides, or Pripyat in Ukraine, abandoned because of a nuclear explosion, Binnend, what a name! Centralia in Pennsylvania where an underground fire raged for decades, Dhaka on the Ganges Delta—'

Fin's cool grey eyes are again brightly glistening.

'—and soon, of course, Miami.'

Daniel looks hard at Fin. The awe Daniel felt for Fin earlier returns like a wave braving the beach, briefly sizzles, retreats again. *How does Fin know the names of all these places and locations but* not *know who Princess Diana is?* Daniel thinks. *How old is Fin? Why can't I seem to tell? Why is* everything *here so difficult to pin down?*

'But at the same time, there's a difference,' Fin says.

'There is?'

'Yes,' Fin nods, 'because *your* town had the chance of a comeback – a second life, or a second attempt.'

Daniel, however, looks unconvinced.

'I suppose that's one way of looking at it,' Daniel shrugs, before nevertheless continuing again:—

—It was so strange to hear about the mine's cavities being turned into a defence against the end of the world when those same cavities had once been the centre of Mika's. The mine's closure was already an ending for him. It was the end of his livelihood and the end of his stability – the accident also injured him physically and for a while he was bedridden – so the mine being turned into some kind of fortress against the destruction of the world – a world I don't think he felt like he'd ever really been to - must have been like rubbing salt in the wound.—

—'Literally!' says Fin, cheerily, but then, more seriously, 'The world *is* the end of the world, if you think about it.'—

—Mika never bought the pebbledashed house he lived in for such a long time, or any other property. He probably should have gotten permission to build his patio from somebody, but he never did, and then it didn't matter, because it was gone before it was ever his. Later, much later—

—'I'm sorry I keep repeating that phrase,' Daniel says.
'It's OK,' says Fin. 'Keep going.'—

—when Mika died, not from his injuries but from lung cancer, and I returned home for the last time for his funeral, I came to think that wealth is as much about the ability to materialise loss as it is about accumulation. Then loss takes up its proper space in the world - then loss isn't outrageous in the way it is otherwise, immeasurable but everywhere nonetheless. By the time I got there - I came in a cab from the airport, like Crystal hadn't all those years ago - the government had demolished our still-tilted house and sold the plot on to a developer. Because of the archive, somebody had a mind to build in our town again. The plots up by McDonald's were once again worth something, but all that was left of Mika's belongings were his wallet and the thin wedding band he'd never removed from his finger. I buried the ring because I thought if I wore it, I'd lose it. Mika's body was cremated without a gravestone. That was what he had wanted and that was the end of it.

But I don't think the end is over yet.

But – I'm confusing things.

I—

    —Daniel hesitates.
    'Yes?' says Fin. —

—I think that to say what I'm trying to say, I have to tell you another story. I have to tell you more about Mika.—

    —'The second petal,' Fin says, nodding, 'of the birdsfoot trefoil.'
    'If you like,' says Daniel, still weary despite the Pepsi. *Does Fin not feel sleepy too?* Daniel wonders, thinking back, now, to the afterparty, and to Fin's mansion, and to finding Fin collapsed in a heap in the ditch of the *Ha Ha* – to the ketamine and its heady effects. *It all seems a world away now*, thinks Daniel.
    'The second petal,' Fin repeats, as if to rouse Daniel from a reverie.

'If you like,' says Daniel, roused, 'but Mika's story isn't mine, so I'm not even sure I can tell it properly. The places it goes to are places I've never been and—'

Daniel stops, suddenly saddened by something.

'Would it help,' Fin says, seeing that Daniel is struggling, 'if I told you my theory about this place – about why you and I are where we are right now, sat side by side on this cliff edge?'

'Who has a theory about the place where they live?' Daniel scoffs.

Fin raises an eyebrow.

Daniel blushes.

'I've come to think,' Fin says, carefully, deliberately, 'that where we are right now is a kind of limbo – but not for people. It's not where *people* go when they die. No. It's like a landfill for lost dreams and disappointments, things that never came to be – things that *we* never ended up being. Thoughts that once crossed somebody's mind – throwaway thoughts that once crossed my mind, and now also your mind. My reasons for being here are similar to yours, similar but different slightly. That's why we can be here at the same time – *have* to be, maybe – but that's also why this landscape doesn't make sense, why the air here is brittle and breaking, why the snow doesn't make either of us feel cold and why I know that's a pterosaur flying through the sky but you don't. You don't, or won't, believe me.'

Fin stops. Daniel stays very quiet.

The junky sea sizzles a bit.

'Either you're completely nuts,' says Daniel, 'or you're still high. Or both.'

'I didn't understand either to begin with,' Fin says. 'I too was frantic and confused. But then I settled in, got used to things, acclimatized. I almost forgot ever having arrived – until you turned up and reminded me.'

The head of the birdsfoot trefoil that Fin passed Daniel earlier still sits, stranded from its stem, on the snow-laden ground. Daniel picks it up and again fiddles with it. One of its petals has now disappeared. The remaining petals seem to have shifted colour; they're no longer the same yellow they were previously, *but perhaps that's just because the flower is dying*, Daniel thinks.

'For a while I thought everything here was real,' Fin continues, one eye on the flower Daniel's fumbling, 'and it is, in a way. In any case, I know how it feels. I too have been in your shoes.'

'I don't believe you,' Daniel says.

'Two moons,' Fin whispers. 'There were two crescent moons in the sky earlier. Think about it. That second moon you could never show Crystal – it's *here*, where we are. Or at least, it was until recently. Maybe if you stay long enough you'll see it again.'

'I don't believe you,' Daniel stubbornly repeats, though this time more tentatively, with a little less conviction.

'No,' says Fin, 'I know you don't. But you're going to carry on anyway. You're going to tell me more about Mika, aren't you? And you're right, by the way. By telling me more about Mika you'll edge closer to whatever it is you're *really* here to say.'

And then, in a different tone, a tone that Daniel hasn't heard before now – 'I hope so, anyway.'

'Yes,' Daniel replies, persuaded to keep going without really knowing why. *Maybe it's because of Fin who is*, Daniel thinks. *But who is Fin?* Out at sea, the cruise ship whimpers and bleats. Stray Tupperware lids tickle her recovering sides; fresh snow lilts on the lids like licked icing. 'Yes,' Daniel repeats, without even meaning to speak – it's as if some unknown force has entered Daniel's voice, and so Daniel has no choice, now, but to keep going, to return to the moment just before the Great Subsidence caused by – *but I'm no longer that kid who blamed Crystal for everything,* Daniel thinks, before beginning again:—

II

—At work alone there were two of them. Two *George Michaels*. There right in front of him in the queue for the hoist, the lift that took the miners down underground, stood the other one. He was holding his helmet against his hip and gobbing spit, wobbly thick, to the quick wind. Without snow to tease, the wind took the spit gladly. He was younger, the other George Michael, and everybody just called him *George* or *Pudding* so that at first he, George Michael the older, had not known of him.

He himself (but he was not himself) was known as *Mike* or occasionally *Mika*, though neither of those names were his real name.

Nor was *George Michael*, he thought.

He shuffled his feet. Fingered the bitty deeps of his pockets. The sky was grey and cumbersome. Unshifting. The stubborn sky would not let go off its load and his real name was unknown to him. His real name was a word he had never heard and never would, because whenever it occurred to him that it existed, that it could possibly exist, he shoved the thought away, buried it.

He wore the same orange kit as George the younger and all the others, trousers slashed by fluorescent strips, a jacket fastened by plastic popper buttons. In it, his body softly heaved.

He shuffled his feet. It was cold, but not as cold as it should have been – not cold enough, no, for snow to come. Behind him, back past the corrugated offices, was the wide road and on the other side of it, the pebbledashed house three along from the one where he'd lived as a kid, where his own kid would soon be waking. Ever since his half-sister's girl had arrived, his kid had taken to sleeping on the settee in front of the T.V., and wearing sunglasses.

Then yesterday when he'd returned home, he'd found the settee gone, vanished. Where it had once been, his half-sister's girl stood.

She had just grinned at him.

He did not know what to make of the sunglasses thing, or he did, but he did not know what to say of it.

In a moment or so the door of the hoist would scuttle and shift, and he himself (but he was not himself) would disappear. His body would go back down below, leaving the cold unfathomable world behind.

George Michael the younger gobbed again. This time the spit hit the gravelly ground. He wondered why they called him *Pudding*. He was small and skinny with home-bleached hair, almost the same orange as his clothes, but then Mika—

—'I'll keep calling my dad *Mika*,' says Daniel, 'because that was how Crystal always referred to him.'—

—often missed the meaning of words. He often had troubles with them. When he was little and slow to speak, some words had totally stumbled him. Funnily enough, though it had not been funny then, one such word was *nobody*, which little Mika had heard as *knobhead*, and *knobhead* was how he'd said *nobody*.

No-bod and *knobheady*.

It had caused him huge embarrassment. Embarrassment was like going underground and not being able to go underground at the same time.

The queue of men was moving forwards now. He patted his flask and the fasteners of his bag, moved along with them. Beneath them, the gravelly ground rattled a bit.

It – little Mika's inability to tell the difference between *knobhead* and *nobody* – had been the perfect opportunity for the kids who already instinctively hated him to hate him more, and then one of them had brought into school a slack length of rubber (the thought of it made him think of the hoist ahead, the traction belt that held its descent) and whipped him with it. To his horror, he had been thrilled by it.

Knobhead. I'm *knobheady*.

These days his own kid hated him.

These days his speech no longer wore him on its sleeve, or no longer bore his secrets on its sleeve – he never could figure out that funny expression – and Mika was mostly quiet at work. He let it be thought that he was simple in the sense of uncomplicated. He let it be thought that he was wholesomely home-grown, not the son of the son of an immigrant. Half the inhabitants of this heart-sinking town were, after all, though that never stopped them from bigotry. He had always meant to leave, but never had – had just never got round to it, though then his own wife had.

He was nearing the lift's threshold now. George Michael the younger swirled suddenly round, scowled at him. What for? Had he caught his heels?

Swirled back again.

This heart-sinking town had been Mika's home since he'd moved here as a kid with his mama and dad and older half-sister. Their house was small and shimmery with dust from the road, which back then had been busy, sometimes heaving, but it was better than where they had lived before. Better than that tall grotty house in the middle of the city. Here there had been fields and views and prospects too, or steady jobs at least. No religion to begin with nor pubs neither, just low hedges and foundations and empty playgrounds.

'The place looks abandoned, not fancy and new,' his dad had scoffed when they'd first arrived.

Both of his parents were dead now.

His half-sister was too, lost to the booze, but Mika was steady. Yes, he thought, he was not who he was not, he was exactly who he was as he stepped into the metal frame of the—

> —'I've forgotten the name for it,' says Daniel.
> '*Hoist*,' says Fin.

—which was the lift that let the miners down underground. He was himself (but he was not himself).

He breathed in a last breath of fresh unsalty air. Then the stubborn sky shut – he caught sight of that last sassy wink of it – and the lift began its shaky descent. George Michael the younger was stood close behind him now. Somebody, not him, was humming something. Above the reluctant moan of the moving lift, Mika could hear somebody humming something.—

> —'What was the tune?' asks Fin.

—He didn't recognize it.

Mika couldn't sing, not for the life of him. When he tried to hum along to a jingle or tune, the notes that came out of his mouth were always beside themselves, not quite what they should have been.

Not that he tried to sing often. But he had done, until he realized how he sounded. How the world heard him.

The lift shuttled on downwards. It was pitch dark inside it now. He thought again of his kid and the fandango of the sunglasses. The glasses were plastic, cheap, and too big, looked stupid and lurid and at the same time, ridiculously fragile, but his kid insisted on wearing them constantly. His kid was smart but crazy. Too smart, maybe. Cleverer, definitely, than that girl was. At her, Mika could hardly bear look. He knew that was cruel but he couldn't help it, couldn't bring himself to do otherwise. He hadn't wanted her to come at all, but in the end he hadn't had much of a choice.

She was his responsibility now, the government had said. They'd sent him a letter explaining.

Like a bill.

Dear Mr. George Michael.

The humming stuttered, then ceased. The hoist fell silent save for the sound of the machinery and the muffled ruffle of close material. Mika immediately missed the lilt of the humming. It had been a sad tune but he liked music, liked hearing it even if it was alien to him. Fancy being completely tone deaf and having a name the same as George Michael. But then, fancy actually *being* George Michael, he thought. Fancy being known of. Fancy being heard of. The only person who'd ever really known him was the mum of his kid, and look what that had come to. Look how that had ended.

How many years was it now since she'd left?

Two.

No three.

His kid had watched plenty of T.V. before she went, then afterwards endlessly. Before she'd left it was always fantasies and animated cartoons. Afterwards, soap operas. He watched them too from the other end of the settee, its sagging cushions padding the tension between them. He'd sometimes felt like they were sat at either end of a seesaw and that he was weighing his side down, down into the ground, while his kid hovered weightlessly at the high end.

He'd bought the deckchair on sale from the store next door to Toys 'R' Us. What was the shop called? He couldn't recall. He'd driven straight there without saying a word to the girl, determined to buy a replacement settee immediately, without blinking, without giving in to her, but then when he was there he had been unable to choose, or unable to make himself part with the money. Both, he thought.

'Can I help you? somebody had said to him, and then he had spotted the deckchair.

God knew what kind of influence the girl was having. God knew what else she and his kid had got up to, he thought, as the lift shimmied and shook, though maybe he shouldn't worry so much. Maybe despite it all some kind of good would come of having a girl around.

His kid—

The lift shimmied—

His kid was always being took for a boy, looked just like a boy, but wasn't one.

The hoist spat out a sharp cracking sound, then carried on rapidly downwards. No matter how many times Mika took this ride, it always startled him. Left him slightly dazed. Made him squeeze his fingernails into his palms, denting them, artificially dimpling them.

No-bod and *knobheady. Fucking—*

George Michael the younger's chest pressed against his back, compelled by the force of the lift's descent.

Fell away again.

He knew he was a hypocrite.

He knew it.

He had not seen his half-sister for ten years or more before she died. He hadn't been able to stand the wild flight of her eyes, the way they blistered, no blustered, stoked by the booze, eyes that couldn't express their own kindness. He and she had once been so close. She had looked after Mika when he was little, during the times when mama was too consumed by work and the possibility of its loss properly to care for him, and during the times when he came home from school crying fat bubbly tears. During the times when he could still cry.

George Michael the younger grumbled something.

Shut up again.

His half-sister's name (he said it under his breath) was Di, short for Diana—

> —'Like the princess,' says Fin.
>
> 'Who,' says Daniel, '*you've* somehow never heard of.'
>
> Fin's head tilts inquisitively. Daniel hiccups on account of the Pepsi, continues:—

—and she had looked like Mika even though they were only half-siblings, not whole, or no, that was the wrong way round, he thought. It made more sense to say that *he* had looked like Di, because Di was the older one. His dad was not her dad. His dad had never got over that fact, had never forgiven Di for something that wasn't her fault, which was just the fact that their mama had once slept with another man.

Or perhaps it was the fact that mama had had a life before them – a life before

Mika's dad, beyond him – that he couldn't stand.

Mika's dad, like Mika now, had ridden this ride deep underground. His dad too had gone to work at the salt face.

But he was dead now. His dad wasn't anybody's dad now – but then that was pretty much how it had always felt, he thought. He had always been the heavy silent type, moustached exactly like Mika was now, curly haired, hard-working and sullen. Almost a cliché, were it not for the twists and turns in his – what was the word for it?—

—'Backstory,' suggests Fin.—

—Yes, that was it, *backstory*. His failed flight abroad when he was still a teenager, then his marriage to mama, much older than he was, his return to the North, to the deathbed of Mika's granddad, who had always refused, point-blank, to tell his kids and grandkids where he came from – where he himself had been born.

'What's it matter to you?' Mika's dad had reported him as saying. 'It's where you're headed that matters. It's where you're *going*.'

Point-blank, now what did that mean? he wondered. Where did a phrase like that come from?—

—'It's when something is shot at very close range,' says Fin. 'Or that's what it once meant.'—

—Something to do with shooting, he thought.
But how did he know that.
He could feel George the younger's quickening breath on his neck.
The lift continued on downwards.—

—'I think,' Fin says, 'that you're getting the hang of this.'—

—Di, short for Diana. Into the grumbling swoon of the descending lift, Mika muttered her name again under his breath. His dad had disliked her whatever she did, however much she'd tried to please to him. The more Di had tried, the more she'd displeased him. He'd never allowed her a decent go at life. But he'd never really let go of her either. There was that time that he'd threatened to beat up an ex-boyfriend when he found out he was bothering her.

Jealousy, Mika thought, suddenly understanding.

The lift stuttered—

Mika just about caught his balance—

Yes, a kind of loveless love for her. Must men always love that way, he wondered. Because of it, Di had never been able to believe herself worth something. Then later, after her illness, came the boozing. Everybody boozed of course, Mika did too, but Di had gone somewhere else with it. Another place, another level. The smudged broken skies of her blue painted eyelids. Mika could still remember the lines of the folds in them. After a while – after watching Di grab her own kid by the wrist and scream into her creased fluffy face, after finding Di asleep on the littered floor of her kitchen again – he had distanced himself. He could have tried to help, but he couldn't – not again. He'd been there, done that, didn't want to go back, and anyway, despite Mika's urging, Di had chosen to have the child of a man who'd left her almost as soon as he'd found out that she was pregnant.

The flashy DJ, his suit everywhere covered in pin-badges.

Crystal's father.

Mika's own kid knew almost none of this. There were many things about Mika his kid didn't know, but most of those things were nothing. A bit of grit in the teeth. Needless to bother with, needless to care about.

Into the unseeing lightlessness of the lift, he grimaced. Bit his lip a bit.

The lift was nearing its low destination now. He unclenched his palms. The cage of the hoist grunted and groaned, then came to a trembling rest. The stuffed bodies shot out of the still-opening doors. Mika let them rush. George Michael the younger slid out past him, his orange hair newly helmeted, his lowslung trousers already showing his bum crevice. Mika chuckled briefly to himself, then followed.

It was like stepping out into a new world.

It was – it was like stepping out into a new world. Always was, every time, a new world that never became old. But at the same time, an old world too, dazzlingly ancient. Or no, he thought, older than ancient. He didn't know the names of all the ages, but he knew halite. He knew the word *salary* came from the word *salt* – he knew that alright. Little Mika might have had his troubles with words, but as a teenager he had read heavily nevertheless, had made his way steadily through books borrowed from the travelling library that traipsed round these new towns, never bothering much, in the meantime, with schoolwork. He knew that salt was once actual wealth, not tiny rectangular paper sachets casually mangled, the granules scattered across McDonald's tabletops. Not just raw material for ridding the roads of their soft heavy burden – not that the roads were ever much burdened at the moment, he thought.

The work they did down here was becoming redundant.

Mika sighed.

Checked his helmet's chinstrap, as was his habit. Kept his gloves off for the time being and ran the flesh of his palm along the salt wall, let the lamp of his helmet flash on it. The salt glittered, little glitters epochs old. Above him, never falling but ever threatening to fall, hung the speleothems.—

> —'Speleothems?' asks Fin.
>
> 'Salt deposits,' says Daniel. 'Some looked like icicles, some looked like straws, and some formed like grabbed handfuls of pop corn.'
>
> Fin looks at Daniel curiously. 'You saw them too? You also went underground?'
>
> 'No,' says Daniel, whose hiccups have momentarily vanished, 'I never went down into the mine. This is just how I imagined it. This is just how I *am* imagining it.'
>
> Fin smiles another wry smile. 'You really are getting the hang of this.'—

—It was like stepping out into a new world, older than ancient. The air was brittle there—

> —'*Here*,' says Fin. 'You have to say *here* if we're inside Mika – if we're seeing things from his perspective, I mean.'—

—The air was brittle here, salty to taste and tight on the lungs but, he thought, good for you. For a long time, salt had been sacred. His thoughts drifted to uses beyond road grit. Water blessed by a sprinkled salt cross became holy and some salt mines had become sanatoriums. Some had been turned into luxury health spas. It made him think of the new gymnasium near to the SnowDome, how the bodies inside made the motions of workers in factories, but with the difference that there they were paying for it.

Fancying paying to be sent deep underground, he thought. Fancying paying to do what he was now doing.

But then again, he had always felt like the mine's atmosphere was good for him. It was true he had a constant cough but that was caused by the tobacco not the salt, though above ground he blamed it on the salt.

A little white lie.

He caught a quick lamp-lit glimpse of George the younger leaping up on to the payloader, the truck that loaded the blasted halite after the explosion and took it back to be crushed, before it was sent up to the world on conveyor belts.

He himself (but he was not himself) was almost old enough to be George Michael the younger's dad, he thought. The dad of the true George Michael had been brutal. But how did he know that? Some documentary on T.V.? Something in *The Sun* maybe?

He let his palm settle on the hard flesh of the salt wall.

It was his job to plant the explosives.

The method was safe, tried and tested. The mine had been mined for half a century or more, though time took on a different significance here. A different – what was the word? *consistency*. It wasn't possible to tell the time this deep underground. There was no weather here and no seasons, though also there were, because the work underground depended upon the coming of snow above ground. The miners needed the sky to break. They needed the sky to let go of its load, or else the mine would close again.

Beneath the dancing beam of his lamp, the salt wall glittered again.

Yes, he thought, the mine had been mined for a long time now. There were cavities that had been left to themselves since the first years of work, where the salt ceiling was trusted, or where the dead who had made it were. The mine was a labyrinth, a series of interlinked chambers, a twinkling bracelet of charms, but he knew his way through it. He knew its rooms as if they were home, knew not to go into the old ones unless it was necessary. Knew just to leave them be, exhausted and done with but there, nonetheless. There, irrevocably.

He checked his chinstrap again. Patted his flask and the straps of his bag. Moved onwards towards the truck that would take him all the way to the salt face, where his work would be done.

The air was brittle and in his broad jacket, his body still softly heaved. Maybe this was how it felt being an astronaut, he thought, a man on the moon, though here there was nowhere to float away. Here was already *away*.

He breathed a salty breath. Hopped up into the truck's passenger seat. The driver briefly nodded at him. *Knobhead* and *nobody. No-bod* and *knobheady*.

Mika nodded back.

The driver turned the key – once, twice, three times in a row – and they set off. Ahead of them trundled the payloader driven by George Michael the younger. The backlights trailed crazy beams on the salt walls. The walls were not white but a grey kind of lilac, sometimes striped with red streaks, which were the fault of old tools that had broken and rusted. Tools long ago abandoned down here, their colours of corrosion slowly strung through the salt walls.

The surface of halite was always sort of trippy, he thought, like a hallucinogen.

Not that Mika knew all that much about hallucinogens. He had never been into drugs, just had no taste for them, though who knew what his own kid would get into. His kid who went about wearing sunglasses constantly, eating McDonald's for breakfast. That was the girl's influence, he thought. He didn't know what to say about any of it. His kid sometimes seemed to him as awkward as he too had once been, but though he had grown out of his awkwardness, settled down on the grim shores of reality, he could tell his kid was the restless kind. It worried him. It was as if his own kid felt the feathery intimacy of the fame that attached to his, Mika's, namesake's name, without actually being—

—'You see?' Fin breaks in. 'Like me. As a kid I used to think I was famous even though I wasn't – even though really I was just an ordinary kid, I believed I was famous, and I behaved that way.'

This revelation silences Daniel. Like the petals of the birdsfoot trefoil, the sea seems now to be shifting in colour: its crests and creases shimmer pink instead of turquoise; its peaks are still tufted with bits and pieces of trash. The sky, too, is whirling with a jumble of colours – it's as if the day where Fin and Daniel are is getting ahead of itself. The sun is sinking more quickly now; the two crescent moons are long gone. The wrecked cruise ship really seems to be recovering – her sides definitely look less damaged, less broken.

'I *thought* I didn't recognise you,' Daniel says quietly, after a bit.

'But at the same time you do, don't you?' Fin replies, quick as a flash.

'What do you mean?'

'You recognise me, even though you don't – even though you've never heard of me. You saw something in me as soon as you got here. Didn't you?'

'I guess you just seemed as if you were somebody,' Daniel says, slowly, cautiously. 'You seemed as if you were famous, I mean. You live in a mansion after all. You have a grand piano in your living room.'

'And a stone sundial.'

At this, Daniel goes quiet again.

'Look,' says Fin, in a breaking voice, a voice almost overwhelmed by its own words, 'When I first arrived I was like you – resistant, bruised. But then – I might as well tell you by this point – I met somebody. Her name was Miss Universe, or at least that was her name in *this* place. I don't remember exactly what we talked about. I remember resting my head in her arms but I don't remember everything I said to her, just bits and pieces, fragments. I'm sure I talked too much – maybe that's why my throat is so sore. We were in some kind of changing room. And we were in Miami, or somewhere that seemed like Miami. Then afterwards, after I left Miss Universe, or after Miss Universe left me,

I felt different somehow. *Here* was different somehow. I wasn't in Miami anymore. I felt as if I'd been famous forever and ever, but I also felt as if the world was ending – as if it *had* ended. I believed I was famous but I didn't believe in the world I was famous within—.'

Fin pauses, flushed. *Funny, Fin seemed so distant and aloof earlier,* Daniel thinks. *Now Fin just seems like anybody else.*

'—and then you turned up on the settee in my living-room. I was annoyed at first. You kept following me around! Now I think I have to hear you out before I can leave – before I can finally leave here.'

Daniel looks blankly at Fin for a moment, then bursts out laughing, which seems a little to hurt Fin.

'That's part of your theory?' Daniel asks, still laughing but trying not to. 'That you have to listen to me say all this before you're allowed to leave here, wherever *here* is?'

Fin sips a last bit of Pepsi, shakes the can, crushes it, then tosses it over the cliff edge. Daniel, too, chugs a last glug of pop and chucks the can down after Fin's. *Funny*, Daniel thinks, *how I'll never hear the aluminium shell meet the sea – how I'll never know, having held it, what happens to it.*

'Yes,' shrugs Fin. 'I think so. I don't think the rules are necessarily stable. I don't think it works the same way for everybody. Why would it? If I'm right and where we are is a mish-mash of lost dreams and disappointments, if this landscape we're inhabiting right now – my mansion, my garden and Ha Ha, the trash-tumbled coastline we were recently walking along, this cliff top – if all this *stuff* is somehow made up of hundreds and thousands of things that never came to be, though at the moment I think where we are is mostly a materialisation of things that never happened for me and increasingly some things that once passed *you* by – then it's bound to be unbelievable. Where we are is bound to be unstable and shifting and unpredictable. It *has* to be – doesn't it?'

Daniel, having listened, thinks for a bit. 'You told me you'd been here as long as that cruise ship. Is *that* true? Is that real?'

But Fin just sighs and shrugs again.—

—There his thoughts went again. Down here underground Mika's thoughts always seemed to shiver and twist. Like glittery jittery beams. Like the shivering lift and the leaping lights of the payloader in front of them. The truck driver steered nimbly, but the journey was jolting. The ceiling was low in this part of the mine, the walls rough and close.

He didn't mind. This was where he belonged.

He breathed in. Licked his lips. There the salt was already. There it was again.

Yes, Mika thought, he belonged down here. If the mine closed again he didn't know what he'd do. If the snow didn't come and there was no need for the grit that rid the roads of their horrible obstacle. The weather was definitely worsening. The cold unfathomable world was warming and warming and there was no telling, now, what the sky meant. The old wisdoms had become nursery rhymes, nonsensical, not to be trusted. But then had they ever been otherwise, he thought. He sometimes wondered whether it was all a neat trick to keep the workers, what was the word—

—'Docile?' Fin suggests.

—Yes, he thought, not knowing how he knew that word, *docile*, dreamy, dream-ridden. The idea that somewhere over the rainbow certainty existed, had existed and would exist, was a fantasy, a complete charade, but it was something to work for. It was something to keep going for. A promise of something, but a sly one.

Though salt taught you otherwise, he thought. Sometimes unresisting (such was salt when it was *fine*, he thought), sometimes hard (such was salt when it was *coarse*), salt was not what it seemed. Where the mine was had once been deep seas, but he was himself (but he was not himself).

The truck rumbled onwards.

It would be another ten minutes or so before the tunnel opened up and they reached the salt face, where the men would set to work drilling the holes ready for Mika's explosives. His kid would be up and about by now, he thought. Above ground the day was unfolding. On his way out of the house he had slid past the kid fast asleep in the deckchair, felt angry, felt fondly. For once, the sunglasses had not seemed absurd.

He knew and he didn't know. He had done his best when his wife left. She hardly telephoned now.

It was his job to plant the explosives.

He had to concentrate.

He had done his best when his wife left, but increasingly he hadn't known how to speak to the kid, hadn't known what to do except sit watching T.V., endless episodes of *Neighbours* and *Home & Away*, where the weather was always the same, sun-kissed, consistent. In the ad break after *Home & Away* – he closed his eyes and saw the sun setting on the lush unlittered beach, heard the tune that accompanied the credits, realized, now, that that was what had been hummed in the hoist, the theme tune for *Home & Away*, or was it? – afterwards, after the credits rolled on Summer Bay, his kid had seen an ad for the SnowDome, the indoor ski-slope where the snow wasn't true. His kid had wanted to go, but it was too costly, and it was also, he'd thought, somehow an insult.

Somehow insulting to him.

He'd made the kid sorry for asking. Given out that same look of disdain he couldn't help but give his half-sister's girl whenever she tried to talk to him. It was the same look his wife had given him before she'd left. It was a look that looked away from the body it was given to. It said *how could you*, without saying anything.

He had always thought that she would come back eventually, his wife, or at least call for the kid, ask for custody. But she hadn't.

He saw, suddenly, the patterns of his life.

Suddenly unsaw them.

Like a Magic Eye puzzle. His kid had a whole book of those. *Magic Eye: A New Way of Looking at the World*, was the title.

The truck lurched.

Maybe he just should have taken his kid to the SnowDome after all, he thought. The snow in the SnowDome was untrue, but the same as true snow essentially. They replicated it by simulating the conditions of clouds – he wasn't sure how – but the snow in the SnowDome didn't need gritting. It didn't keep the mine open. It was snow like snow in the plastic sphere of a snowglobe, transfixing and pretty and inconsequential. But maybe, he thought, that was OK. Maybe he should have taken his kid anyway. Maybe he just should have found the money and agreed to go to – maybe that would have said something.

The truck lurched again. Jittery beams. Above him, salt, to his sides, salt, beneath him, salt. Salt of the earth, salt grit, sanatoriums.

He coughed.—

>—Now Daniel can feel hiccups threatening again.
> 'Hold your breath,' Fin suggests.
> 'I can't,' Daniels says. 'I have to keep going.'—

—He had to concentrate.

Across the entire crust of the globe, across time, there were salt mines. Salt lakes where the method of extraction was evaporation via great expanses of saltpans, not underground and mechanical like here. Mines in Belarus owned by the same company that had once tried to buy this one from the government. Now, Mika thought, they wouldn't bother. China. Pink salt from the red hills near Khewra, where the foreman's forefathers had moved from to help modernize the old slip-shod mines, taking back what colonialism had taken from them, or trying to. He didn't know, not completely, what had brought them here. Siberia where the mines had been worked by forced labour and then of course there was America, which was, he thought, a continent made by mining, of matter and of bodies, bodies extracted and made into property, disrupted from their environs and—

—'Wait,' Fin says. 'Did Mika really think this?'

'No,' Daniel replies, with a new confidence, a refreshed resolve, if also a residue of hesitancy. 'I'm making him think this. I'm making him see things he didn't necessarily see –though I also need you to see his unseeingness. His contradictions and reflex resistances and—'

Daniel stops.

'Yes?' prompts Fin.

'It's just that I think I'm beginning to understand something about Mika that I didn't before. The reason Crystal called him a *hypocrite* and why he was so cruel to her. Either that, or I'm just fantasising – making it up to make up for something I'll never fully understand.'

Where Fin and Daniel are, snow falls.

'I don't think there's necessarily a difference,' Fin says, long eyelashes fluttering snowflakes.

'Between understanding and fantasising?' says Daniel, before adding, without waiting for an answer, 'But the truth still matters. It *has* to. Doesn't it?'—

—He had heard of disused mines being turned into theme parks. Conveyor belts had been transformed into slides for consumers to ride and once down inside, the punters walked, gobs wide, beneath salt chandeliers, cooed delicate statues sculpted by the chiselled bodies of dead miners, prayed in chapels and were taken on ticketed tours through cavernous rooms where they were shown the huge chunky salt pillars, which kept the ceiling up. At the tour's end, the tourists received a trinket, a keepsake, a *crystal*.

Mika coughed again.

The driver of the truck raised an eyebrow.—

—'At what? says Fin. —

—At nothing, as far as Mika could tell.

Magic Eye: A New Way of Looking at the World. His kid had complained about not being able to do the puzzles, about never being able to see through to the other side of them. Once, Mika had picked the book up from the kitchen table and tried. The psychedelic pattern he'd happened upon had instantly transformed before his eyes, but he hadn't liked the feeling, the funny feeling it gave him. It had felt like a memory of something but a memory of nothing, something that had never entered the world. A world that never became a world.

That was exactly what it was like down here, he thought, a world that never became a world.

Not long, now, to the salt face.

He checked his chinstrap again. Ahead of the truck trundled the payloader, driven by George Michael the younger, Mika's *could have been* kid, his *might have been* son. He could sense the lad's impatience even from a distance. He felt as if he could anyway. George Michael the younger with his home-bleached hair, and hint of a bum crevice. *Knobhead* and *nobody. No-bod* and *knobheady*.

Fucking—

It irritated Mika but it delighted him too, the thought of a mine as a theme park. Sometimes, when the work was long and the salt deep in his lungs, he would take to imagining the mine as his mansion—

>—'Like me again,' Fin says. 'See? There's some kind of affinity between us. Even though you and I are complete strangers, there's something between us that means *Never Was* can endure while we're both here together.'
>
>'*Never Was*? What's *Never Was*?' Daniel asks.
>
>'Here, of course. This place. This landscape. This world, if it is a world.'
>
>Daniel attempts to swallow another hiccup, but it gets up and away anyway. Out

of Daniel's mouth along with the hiccup comes a bubble, pink and rubbery-looking.

'I thought you didn't believe in the world,' Daniel says, watching the bubble be buffeted by snowflakes. 'In any case, I'm talking about Mika, not myself. Like I said, this is Mika's story, not mine.'

'But you're talking about yourself too,' Fin says, 'Mika's story is also yours – or at least, it's a necessary perspective on it.'

Daniel reaches forwards, stabs the pink bubble with a pointed finger.

'Crystal used to blow bubble gum bubbles,' Daniel says moodily, changing the subject, 'when she wasn't smoking.'

'I know,' Fin says.

'*How* do you know?' snaps Daniel. 'How could you possibly know that? I haven't mentioned it till now. I left that detail out!'

'How did *you* know about the speleothems in the salt mine?'

Both Fin and Daniel stare out to sea. 'That bubble you just hiccupped up,' Fin says, trying again, 'what if I said it belonged to Crystal once? What if I said the air it contains once circulated through her lungs? What would you think then?'

'I'd think,' Daniel replies, eyes on the rubbishy tufts of sea either side of the recovering cruise ship, 'that you were trying to convince me Crystal had been here too. That wherever we are now is somehow—'

Daniel pauses, looks for the right word, finds it in the flotsam surfing the sea's foam:

'—*littered* with Crystal's lost dreams and disappointments too. I mean, I wouldn't put it past you to try and convince me of such a thing. It's no crazier than anything else you've said.'

'But wouldn't that help to explain things?' Fin replies, smiling. 'If Crystal had been to *Never Was* too, wouldn't that make some kind of sense to you?'

But instead of answering, Daniel continues:—

—He knew the mine's rooms by heart, after all, could have called the chambers ballroom one and ballroom two, carved hallways connecting all the salt mines across the crust of the globe, made them all *his*—

—'Like some kind of subcutaneous colonialist,' Fin says. —

—but Mika wasn't one for parties. He liked music but he couldn't sing and he couldn't dance, not for the life of him. Funny then, he thought again, to share a name with somebody famous for singing and dancing. Somebody who was somebody, whose body appeared on T.V. moving in time and in rhythm with itself. Somebody whose body danced across screens, even when really, that same body was sleeping.

But why now did his thoughts jitter and drift like this, he thought.

He was disciplined. He was consistent.

He leant back in the plastic seat of the truck, concentrated on the task ahead.

It was his job to plant the explosives. The men would drill the holes into the hard salt rock, and then he would feed in the pellets, carefully, stealthily. The method was safe, tried and tested, but Mika worried nevertheless. Even after all these years of working down here, he couldn't help worry some. *Stop being such a—*

But he had held himself (but he was not himself) together for so many years.

Stop being such a pussy about it.

He had gotten into an argument with one of the foremen a few years ago, not long after his wife had left. It had been neither wise nor pretty. The younger miners were careless and reckless, Mika had claimed. They moved too quickly and rushed things, forgot to double-check the equipment and machinery or just didn't bother. Expected it all to be fine because it always was. Mika thought such arrogance tempted fate. The foreman had told him to stop being so superstitious, that speed was a good thing. *Stop being such a fucking pussy about it*, the foreman had said, which had made Mika's cheeks flare, and then he had called the foreman two regrettable words.

Tried and tested

It wasn't far, now, to the salt face.

He licked a salty lip.

In the past, after Mika had finished planting the explosives, the miners had retreated back up to the surface of the world, to wait for the explosion, to be sure to be safe from it. Now they didn't bother. Now they just travelled backwards horizontally, crouched under the crazed crowd of speleothems, let the trigger be pressed and waited. Mika considered this new way of working to be the foreman's revenge. The foreman himself stayed above ground – of course he did. Mika would have done just the same, could he have done. He hated being bossed but he wasn't a union-type, had never been a member of any club in his life, had no interest in feeling part of something. He was too far apart from everything.

Too old.

Out of it.

Ancient.

It wasn't far, now, to the salt face.

The son of the foreman's brother-in-law was called *Ace*. Ace's dad worked over at the elevator factory. Mika bristled at the thought of the elevator factory. Thinking of it made him think of the mine closing and having to mope across town asking for work that wasn't his own, work that didn't have his name on it. Not any one of his names on it. The older he got the harder that was, the more embarrassing.

Embarrassment was like—
Stop being—
He had sometimes seen Ace stood waiting for George Michael the younger after a shift, outside the clubhouse, his feet shyly shuffling the gravelly ground, his hair perfectly curtained. What kind of name was that, *Ace*? Mika wondered. What was it short for?

He remembered.

Aysar. His kid brother was Baahir.

But how did he know that?

Stop being such a—

He put the thought of the foreman out of his head. The truck had now come to an abrupt stop behind the payloader. They had arrived, at last, at the salt face. Mika jumped down from the passenger seat. His knees winced upon impact but he ignored the pain. He was used to it. Here in the large cavity there were long lustrous lamps on the ground, giving off light like the light on a film set. Or light like he imagined a film set as having. The salt walls seemed to soar as a result, and the ceiling was higher here.

Mika glanced briefly up at it.

Looked about for the lad manning the machine that drilled the holes into the salt face.

Saw him and hailed. The lad waved happily back. Mika went over and spoke something quietly to him. The lad was growing a moustache, he noticed, but it was fluffy still. Not coarse and flourishing, like Mika's.

The *Home & Away* theme tune drifted into his head.

Petered quickly back out again.

The lad powered the drill on. Mika stepped back and pulled some muffs from his bag, carefully fitted them over the round of his helmet. From the corner of his eye he caught sight of George the younger doing the same. He fumbled grumpily with the muffs before fitting them. Funny, Mika thought again, how there were two of them, two *George Michaels* deep underground in the same salt mine. He wondered suddenly if it ever bothered him, the other George Michael, being called what he was, whether it made him feel strangely shadowed, somehow touched by a life that wasn't his.

He thought again of his kid and the sunglasses.

Thought (but it was hard for him even to think of her name) of Crystal. The way she crashed through the house in her white socks and high heels, a long lost echo of her mum's movements three doors down. An echo that had neglected to echo until now. She couldn't stay with him and his kid forever, he thought. She would have to go again at some point – she was, what, sixteen, nearly seventeen – and maybe when she left his kid would be OK, maybe then things would go back to normal. The same stiffened stilted old ordinary. Maybe then everything would be OK, because when Crystal went there would be less to remind him of what wasn't there, what had not come to be.—

—'What never was,' Fin nods.

—The drilling began. Mika watched.

Manning, he thought, that was another funny word. He'd sometimes wondered why it was always men who dug graves, why men were always pallbearers at funerals. Why did it seem unseemly somehow, the thought of being buried by a woman?

He watched the drills reach out to the salt face. A slow steady approach, then a puncturing. The muffs did a good job of softening the sound.

He adjusted them nonetheless.

He had not gone to his own half-sister's funeral. Hadn't been able to bring himself to. The feeling of not being able to go had been similar to the feeling of not being able to visit her when she was still living, not being able to bring his finger to pull the final digit of her phone number in the phone's wheel or to answer when he felt, could just tell, it was her on the other end – and in that sense, it occurred to him now, as the drill shrilly drilled despite the muffs covering his earholes, Di's death had not mattered much. It hadn't made that much of a difference to him.

He saw, suddenly, the patterns of his life. Suddenly unsaw them. *No-bod* and *knobheady. Fucking—*

He watched the drills drive into the salt face.

He knew she had been cremated. He knew that at least. She could have been buried here – there were as many vacancies in the cemeteries as there were empty building plots – but she hadn't been. He wasn't even sure, hadn't asked the priest who'd handled her funeral, where her ashes were scattered. Maybe somewhere she liked, like the seaside, he thought. He remembered a trip with her to the holiday park by the sand dunes, with the nightly cabaret and that other, gruffer, salty sea air, and towards the end, an infestation of flying ants.—

—'What was the name of the holiday park?' Fin asks.—

—Pontin's.

He could still see in his mind the sight of the ant swarm descending, gently touching the flat tops of the chalets, ascending again.

Almost apocalyptic, he thought. That was how it had felt at the time. Years later he'd read that flying ants were just ordinary ants that had sexually matured. They grew little wings and flew when the weather became humid.

Their *nuptial flight*, it was called.

Three years, now, since his wife left.

He watched the drills drive—

He had been happy in the first years of marriage. Thrilled actually. The kid had come along and kept them both on their toes, and his wife – she had worked at the elevator factory, but as a secretary – had loved him. He had loved her too, fiercely, too fiercely maybe. She was above him and snobbish but that had made him laugh, and he had quite liked her fastidiousness. Her middle-classy fastidiousness. In time the kid had wearied them both. He had found himself becoming morose and then, to his surprise and bewilderment, he had felt like his mind was going back in time, watching the kid grow up. He had always thought that it would be the opposite. He'd thought having a kid would fling him into the future headfirst irreversibly, but it hadn't been like that.

It hadn't helped that they lived three up from the house that Mika had mostly grown up in, the pebbledashed house his dad and mama had died in, the same house his half-sister Di had lived in and left, come back to again, left again.

So many times, she'd had a go at things.

He watched the drills drive into the salt face.

Di short for Diana, like the princess. Paparazzi motorbikes, eyes swimming in sadness. Fish out of water.

He saw and unsaw the patterns of his life.

He had done his best to stop the avalanche. For a long time – a decade – before Di's death, he had stopped speaking to her at all, had not wanted to deal with her drunkenness, considered himself (but he was not himself) done with the habits he had found himself having between the years of sixteen and twenty, which were the years of his life when Di had returned to live again at home, having attempted to hold down her own household and job, but then having become ill. Having mysteriously collapsed. She was, what, maybe twenty-five at the time, almost ten years older than him.

Almost thirty by the time she left home again.

When was the last time he had said her name out loud, he thought. When was the last time that the world had heard of her.—

> —'*Kleos*,' repeats Fin, 'means both fame and the way the fame is communicated.'
> 'Yes,' says Daniel. 'You've said that.'—

—His muffs muffled the sound of the drilling machine.

For the first year or so of Di's return home, it had been him, teenage skinny Mika, who had nursed her. It had been him who had held her weak bony hand as it littered white flakes of eczema onto the sheets of the bed they'd once shared, like she had held little Mika's when he was tiny and tearful. Stupidly, during that time, he had come to think of himself as her bodyguard. She had seemed so incredibly delicate and he had wanted, so much, to take care of her. He had imagined the sheets of the bed as crisp shifting layers of snow, snow that had come from the dry skies of her body.

Her brittle clouds.

He half-laughed, now, to think of that.

His muffs muffled the sound of the drilling machine.

If the mine closed again he'd be forced to take lorry jobs, or else ask at the elevator factory.

He couldn't afford to keep Di's girl for too long, he thought. He made her name take shape on the tip of his tongue – *Crystal*. The shape sliced his tongue's skin, tasted sharp to him. The letter from the government had said she'd been excluded from school. *What for?* he'd wondered and then he had read on. There were multiple reasons but among them one that had caught his attention. Crystal had lured a boy into repeatedly smacking her one, had somehow succeeded in convincing him to punch her hard in the face until she bled, and then claimed the attack had been unprovoked. The letter hadn't said *smacking* but *lured* was the word the letter had used, and Mika had stumbled on it. It had seemed—

A kind of loveless love for her.—

Somehow unfair to him.

The drill drilled.

Salt of the earth, salt grit, sanatoriums.

Cabarets and sand dunes.

Disturbed was another word the letter had used. It must have been before Di's death that Crystal had been excluded from school, he thought.

Afterwards would surely have been cruel.

The drill drilled.

He himself (but he was not himself) was being cruel to her.

He knew it.

He knew it but couldn't do anything about it. The girl's arrival had felt like a nightmare to him. He'd felt as if she was coming for him, calling for him from somewhere whose existence he didn't want to acknowledge, a shadow not his, just obstinately attached to him.

The drill drilled.

Of the girl's own grief, Mika didn't want to know. He had enough to worry about.

If the mine closed again he'd be forced to take lorry jobs.

For a long time during the time when she'd come back to the house, having mysteriously collapsed, Di had hardly put a foot down on the flowery-patterned carpet. She had been too scared to. Its softness was false and untrustworthy, she'd said, and Mika had felt like he'd known what she meant by that. Somehow he'd understood. For days on end, she had stayed in bed. The doctor who had eventually come out to visit her had said it was nothing, that Di was just making it up. Mika's dad had silently touched his moustache, and mama had hurriedly nodded. There was nothing wrong with her, everybody kept saying after that. It was not that Di *could* not get out of bed but that she *would* not, everybody kept saying, which was a difference that had struck Mika as stupid, because what did it matter whether Di *could not* or *would not*, he'd thought, when she wasn't getting up out of bed either way.

Then when she had done, when she'd leant against his body and they'd walked together up the road to the spot where the McDonald's now stood, he had felt crushed by the weightless weight of her, heavier than herself.

He watched the drills drive into the salt face.

Thought again of his kid and the sunglasses, the settee, the deckchair. His kid was thirteen now, smart, but a slow starter. Was always being taken for a boy but wouldn't be for long. He knew and he didn't know.

Di had stayed in bed for a year or more. Mika had taken her her food, and sometimes read to her. —

—'What did he read to her?' asks Fin. —

—He couldn't remember. She had slept a lot. Eventually she had gotten up and found a job in a shop in town, in the grey angular shopping centre that back then was busy, often heaving, and for a while she had become lifelike again. Their pebbledashed house by the side of the wide road was once again filled by the outrageous fun of her. The heady unsteady vim of her. Mika had been thrilled by her recovery, but his dad had hated her all the more for it. He had taken it as proof she'd been faking, called her a liar and a leech, couldn't stand to hear her laugh ricochet through the papery walls, wouldn't eat with her.

Then he had given her some kind of ultimatum.

Mika had fantasised about confronting him. What has she done to you? What have you done to her?

But then – just like that – his dad had had his heart attack. Just like that, the man's heart had gone under.

Mika had discovered him slumped on the settee, a glass of vodka tipped up beside his limp wrist, his lap soggy from the spilt drink or possibly from piss – Mika hadn't been able to tell the difference from a distance, and he hadn't gotten up close. Hadn't wanted to touch him.

His unliving body.

He should have called for the ambulance instantly, but he hadn't done.

He'd waited a bit.

The drill shrilly drilled.

Mika scratched at his face.

His eyes had stayed drier than dry, the day his dad died, but mama had cried as if she really must have loved him, as if some obscure part of her heart had lived off his disgust for Di, her own daughter. As if her old man's undisguised hatred of Di had given her something he couldn't otherwise give her, not directly. Mika wasn't sure when exactly Di's drinking had worsened, but he thought it must have been around then, after his dad's death, when Di must have realised, on account of her reaction, where mama's allegiances lay.

Where her love lay.

Was that how women were destined to love, he wondered. Brutally, ruthlessly.

It was when you understood you were

still capable of being in the world despite it all that the world became truly unbearable, he thought.

He watched the drills drive into the salt face.

Thought again of his kid and the sunglasses.

He knew and he didn't know, yes, because during those years between sixteen and twenty he himself (but he was not himself) had fallen away from the world. That was how it seemed to him now, though sometimes the muffled ghost of those years drifted back into his body, and he would remember how it had felt to enter Di's room, which had smelt of lavender laced with bitter bedridden breath, and which was where, when Di was still asleep or just stirring, her eyes barely open to the intolerable light, Mika had chosen, slowly but surely, clothes from her wardrobe, a skirt and a shirt, no, a blouse, and dressed himself (and then he was himself).

That was how he had thought of it, as dressing himself (and then he was himself).

He had known Di had known, even if her eyes remained closed. She had watched him without watching him, understanding or just unbothered. She had looked like him or he had looked like her. The fading sun had briefly tinted the blue wallpaper purple. He had turned his head and in the slim oblong mirror nailed to the wall, seen the feminine fall of her collar soften his jaw, then harden it.

Eventually Di left home again, took most of her clothes, carried on with the booze, moved to the city, got involved with a man Mika couldn't stand, the DJ. Then she gave birth to her girl – to Crystal.

He still remembered the way she had screamed at her.

The drilling was done, and now it was his turn. It was Mika's job to plant the explosives.

He swallowed a salty breath.

Savoured the taste of it.

Unlike many of the other miners, he had never developed an ingrained craving for sweetness – not except Pepsi. Sugar was the opposite and not the opposite of salt. A fuel but a false one, pumped into bloodstreams to accelerate industry, the product of slavery. He had always disliked the lingering feeling of it on his teeth, but he liked Pepsi.

Could have done with some now, mixed with sloppy splashes of vodka.

No, he thought, not mixed with anything.

Though he'd never told anybody, though nobody but Di knew, he wasn't ashamed of having dressed himself in her clothes, or if he was then the shame had quickly frittered away from him, been overtaken with a feeling of – but he had never quite known the word for it. It had put him at ease, the feeling of the material just touching his knees, which back then were still brisk and unbothersome. But it had also shown him his ease didn't exist in the world. It had steeled him for something – he wasn't sure what – but he never had caught sight of the cause of it, couldn't tell what *it* even was, why his body wanted to feel itself – funny, he thought, now approaching the salt face, how words sometimes undid the world, how a body was *itself*, never *herself* or *himself* – out of sync with itself.

Why that little gap or difference made him feel real.

It was his job to plant the explosives.

He was concentrating.

It wasn't that he wasn't a man. Despite the best efforts of the kids at school and the bleak frowns of his dad, he had always known that. He wasn't stupid – he knew that for some it *was* like that – but for him, it wasn't, it was different. It was the drift of a different body through his. It was—

He was feeding the explosives into the holes now. His muscles remembered the action before his thoughts did. Over the years his labours down here had inevitably buffed him. His lean body was strongly contoured.

He felt the sore salted eyes of the other miners upon him.

It was what it was, he thought, that was all, and that was the end of it.

He was feeding the pellets into the salt face. Once they were in, once each hole was filled, he would attach the wires to the blasting cap. There were forty holes altogether in the face, one for each year of his life except four.

Steadily, carefully. The method was safe, tried and tested.

His helmet slipped a little. He paused to adjust it.

To be sure, nobody down here would ever have thought it of him, his having dressed himself in that way. Not moody Mike, not silent Mikey. Most of the miners didn't even know his full name – just like he hadn't known George Michael the younger's until recently – and after his argument with the foreman they all had him down as a fussy old bigot anyway, which was ridiculous, because many of the younger workers were more bigoted than he was, but because they were younger they got away with it. They felt like the world was theirs and somehow, because they felt that way, the world went that way – it somehow became that way.

He sighed.

It was what it was, he thought again, that was all, and that was the end of it. —

—'It fell upon you centuries ago,' says Fin, in a sing-songy voice, 'but you just did not know how to come to it.'—

—But now where did a thought like that come from, he wondered. Maybe he was already dehydrated. The brackish air down here easily did that. It shrivelled his skin and the cells of his brain, sent his mind swirling, curly whirly, a theme park version of itself.

He took a sip from the flask he kept attached to his trousers.

Wished there was vodka in it. Was glad there wasn't.

Carried on working.

Cabarets and sand dunes. Salt grit. Sanatoriums.

The girl had tried to provoke him, he thought, by dumping the settee.

George Michael the younger was out of his payloader, stalking, impatient.

But Mika was concentrating.

At first it had given him nosebleeds, being this deep down underground and concentrating. He would come up in the hoist at the end of a shift, crushed salt crusting his eyelashes, his yellow jacket tied tightly about his waist and the sleeve of his T-shirt all bloodied. He never noticed the nosebleed when it was happening. He'd have wiped his nose on his sleeve without realizing it was bleeding and then, above ground, he would have noticed. Or somebody else would have pointed it out to him. It was funny, the blood, because sometimes returning to the surface of the world at the end of a shift made him feel like a murderer, or like he felt a murderer might feel. Like he'd done something down deep underground that made no sense above ground, something untranslatable, but something that made sense to him. —

—'Like Crystal,' Fin says.
'Yes,' says Daniel. 'In many ways Mika and Crystal were similar, though I never would have thought that at the time, during Crystal's visit. It never would have occurred to me.'—

—He'd almost finished packing in the explosives.
He thought again of those years between sixteen and twenty.
Thought again of his kid and the sunglasses.
He wasn't stupid. He knew, now, just from watching T.V., that things were changing. In some places, in some ways. In the city maybe but not here in this heart-sinking town, not deep underground in a salt mine. Here, time was untouchable. Here underground the time that went by above ground was nothing, a dimple, a crease, a wrinkle.

Knobhead and *nobody*. *No-bod* and *knobheady*. *Fucking—*

He'd almost finished now.

He suspected George Michael the younger of being in love with that lad Ace. Mika was not that way, though for a while, it was true, he had wondered. Then he'd met his wife and fallen in love, and he had been happy. They'd had the kid together. He had expected his happiness to continue to grow, for the future to unfurl like the petals of some seasonless flower, but then his mind had begun travelling back in time, watching the kid grow up. No matter how hard he'd tried to settle down on the shores of reality – no matter how much it seemed like he had done – everything was always on the edge of subsiding, like the ground in the town the best part of his life had been spent in.

He sighed.

The girl had tried to provoke him.

He sighed again.

One early yawning morning before breakfast, his fingertips gently touching the head of the figurine that stood, mermaid-skirted, on the windowsill, his kid's feet stomping the ceiling above him, he had told his wife about his half-sister, Di, and how she had died a living death when he was a teenager. The story had just suddenly rushed out of him. He had told her how Di had mysteriously collapsed and come back home to the pebbledashed house three doors down, become bedridden, gotten better again, and then he had told his wife about his dressing too.

'You *what*?' she'd said, unturning from her work at the cooker, her back blankly staring and staring at him. Then the scrunched profile of her face as she bent over to open a cupboard for something. It was a look that looked away from the body it was given to.

He had not expected to tell her that part of the story. It had just rushed of his mouth, automatically and unrelentingly, like an ad jingle or like the *Home & Away* theme tune.

'It was years ago.'

Her back blankly staring and staring.

'Love, it was centuries ago.'

He had almost finished now. He caught the thick wires in his hand, held them there.

It had given her a reason to leave him. Maybe he had wanted to give her that, he thought. By then it was already bad between them. Afterwards, after he'd told his wife, she'd said she could no longer trust him. She hadn't been able to believe it was true, she'd said, and then she'd not been able to trust him. She'd said she didn't know who he was anymore, who he had ever been. *Queer*, she'd called him, in their final awful argument, as if it was still the worst thing in the world to be called, as if she'd never heard of that word being used differently now. Unlike him and the kid, his wife had never watched that much T.V.

She had left the kid with him when she went, nonetheless.

Funny, he thought.

But why was everything always just *funny* to him.

He had almost finished packing in the explosives.

He wiped his face with his arm, took another sip from the flask he kept attached to his trousers. Sweat brimmed on his eyebrows, trickled over them, stung his eyes on account of the salt in it.

He concentrated.

He had seen them together at a work party, Ace and George Michael the younger. Ace must have been there as the son of the brother-in-law of the foreman. Mika had been sat at one of the circular tables in the clubhouse, picking at his food, squeezing the squeezy bottle of ketchup, not dancing. George the younger was drunk and spinning round and around on the dancefloor, to a tune by the true George Michael no less. 'Don't let the sun go down on me. Although I search myself it's always somebody else that I see.' In his fist was a pint and the beer made glistening spirals as he span. When eventually he slipped in it, as was inevitable, Ace had run lovingly over to him. It was a reflex reaction but revealing, and somebody had chucked their own pint at the two of them.

Blessed by a grim fizzy stickiness, Mika thought.

Cabarets and sand dunes. That holiday with Di to the Pontin's by the seaside.

Flying ants.

Salt grit.

Salt chandeliers.

A deckchair. The apocalypse.

Was that the very same work party Crystal's dad had turned up at, he thought. Was that the same party her dad had DJ'd at? Mika hadn't been able to believe his own blinking eyes at first, hadn't been able to believe he would have had the nerve, but there he was in his silver pin-badge-dappled suit – it was him, definitely. Mika had thought it was some sort of provocation at first, but it was worse, it was just work, and then it seemed that the man had no memory of Mika. Hadn't recognised him.

He had brought his own kaleidoscopic lights, and a glitter ball too.

Mika had made up his mind not to say anything. Then later, much later, when everybody was leaving – despite hating parties, Mika had been among the last to leave, had been unable to make himself return home across the wide road, which at night was like the river Styx, he liked to imagine, though he couldn't have said, had he ever been asked to elaborate, which side of the road lay life and which lay death – he had shared a rollie and last shot with the DJ.

Crystal's dad. What were the chances?

He shoved an explosive deep into a puncture. Not too many more to go now.

Even then – even when it was just the two of them, sharing a last shot and a rollie at one of the circular tables – the bastard hadn't recognised him. He'd even asked Mika his name. Mika had hesitated over his words, knocked back his drink, then answered *George Michael*, which was his full name but not his real name.—

—'Because his real name was unknown to him,' Fin says. —

—'Are you fucking kidding me?' the DJ had answered, his eyes soggy from the booze and softly amused, and then, 'He's dead now, isn't he?' which was news to Mika and as it turned out, news to the world and no news at all, because the true George Michael was alive and kicking. But for a moment, Mika had believed otherwise. For a moment the world itself had been otherwise, though only a little bit. It would be years, still, until the true George Michael would hurl his own body from a moving car, a car travelling down a motorway. Mika would never see that story in *The Sun*, stuck with cellotape to his kid's bedroom wall, which was covered, floor to ceiling, head to toe, in clippings.

At the party, or at its end, Mika had not asked the DJ his name in turn.

Funny, he thought now, that a DJ, of all people, should have gotten mixed up like that. About the death or not-death of George Michael.

Funny, he thought now, deep underground in the rockpit, to think of all the many George Michaels there must have been in the world.

But why was everything always just *funny* to him?

He had finished now. He caught the wires in his hands – wires like wires attached to a torso, as if the sheer salt face was the skin of a body about to be pumped back to life, not destroyed. He tracked the wires back, slowly, to the capsule. The method was safe, tried and tested. His lungs were prickly from the salt and his eyes were dry, tired. He felt like they might have popped had he touched them.

Like blood blisters.

The miners were retreating to the back of the cavity, and then out of it, along the tunnel. The explosion would be neat, precise.

Controlled.

Funny, he thought, what a life was.

Funny how a life was like a body but at the same time, nothing like a body. How those two things needed each other without being equivalents. Funny, he thought now, moving away from the face, how life wasn't possible without a body to live by, but you could have a body without a life, and a life could live on beyond a body. Not necessarily as a ghost – no, a ghost was too substantial, too much of something for what he was thinking of – but just as a sifting sleeting of memories, haphazardly remembered. He had not gone to his own half-sister's funeral, but for years he had kept a porcelain statue of her namesake on the windowsill.

Princess Diana, dressed as mermaid.

Sand dunes and chandeliers.

Sometimes the sun sipped the porcelain water Princess Di swam in. Sometimes he used her as an ashtray.

Why did he do that?

He nodded at the lad whose job it was to control the explosion. Checked his chinstrap. When the miners were at the agreed retreated distance, the lad would set the timer and retreat too. The face would collapse but precisely, exactly as expected, exactly as predicted.

Mika worried nonetheless. Get away, he thought, far away, from the rigged salt face. He jumped back up on the truck. The driver turned the key – once, twice, three times in a row – and they took off.

They ought to have been going all the way back up to the surface of the world, he thought.

But they wouldn't be.

The morning after the work party, the very same one that Crystal's dad had DJ'd at, was the morning he had told his wife about what had happened with Di, and about his dressing. *Queer*, his wife had called him. *The both of you*, she'd said, meaning, he realized now, him and his kid too, who looked like a boy, was always being took for a boy, but wasn't one.

But the kid was just as much hers as his.

He felt suddenly like he'd forgotten something.

Put the thought away.

The *Home and Away* theme tune drifted into his head.

Petered back out again.

A *fucking foreigner*, was what Mika called the foreman during that argument, not long after his wife had left. In turn he'd been called racist and, what was the word—

—'Xenophobe?' says Fin. —

—'*Xenophobe*,' Mika repeated, almost out loud, as the truck rumbled on, its engine blubbering vowels, and probably he was, probably he deserved that. For though the words he'd used could also have been used of his dad and definitely his grandad, Mika had used them on account of the colour of the foreman's skin, and whereas the foreman had been born here, Mika's grandad had not been. But Mika's skin was salt white with wrinkles of pink, and though he didn't feel like that had much helped him, he also knew that that had helped him.

He knew what it had not cost him.

He knew it.

After he had said what he had said, he'd felt desperately ashamed, more ashamed than he'd ever been. But he couldn't take those two words back now. Couldn't breathe the bad tang of them back in.

The lad whose job it was to set off the explosion had started the count down. Were they far enough away? Why had the truck stopped?

His thoughts flipped quickly between hatred and love, love and then hardened old hatred. Then rage, then a softening. Hard and soft, course and fine. Though it feels severe, the other side of abandonment is gradual.

The count went down.

Upon leaving the clubhouse at the end of the party, the DJ, Crystal's dad, what were the chances, cabarets sand dunes cha-cha-chandeliers—

—'Hey,' says Fin, because Daniel is slightly slurring, 'are you OK?' —

—Upon leaving the clubhouse at the end of the party, the DJ had inexplicably swirled around and punched him, hard, in the left eye. Mika hadn't even let on that he knew who he was or what he had done, how his carelessness had made Di's hurting hurt more. But he was glad of the punch, wherever it had come from, because it had caused him to cry involuntary tears, and because he deserved it.

Funnily enough, the eye had never bruised much. The wound had not properly shown itself.

The count went down.

He felt like he'd forgotten something.

Put the thought away.

The count went down.

Sanatoriums.

Cha-cha-chandeliers and—

> —'*Hey,*' Fin repeats, because Daniel's amber eyes are flaring again, becoming bright red, the same colour of the blood on the sleeve of Daniel's T-shirt, which is itself becoming soggy with sweat, unless the wetness is the blood on the sleeve undrying, unless time in *Never Was* is both accelerating *and* reversing, as if the landscape of *Never Was* is somehow in the strange trance that Daniel seems to be entering, as if, as if...
>
> '*HEY!*'—

—chances and sand dunes.

During that holiday with Di to the Pontin's by the seaside, Mika's dad had taken the two of them on a drive one afternoon. For some reason, mama had not come. He couldn't remember, now, where they had driven. There were those remains of a village that had slipped into the sea not far from where the holiday park was, so maybe it was there, he thought. He wasn't sure. But he remembered how, on the return trip to the holiday park, he had been sat in the back, Di in the front in the passenger seat, because she was older. He still remembered the shape that the nape of her neck made. Everybody was quiet. Then – just like that – the mood in the car had changed. Just like that, the weather had worsened. Nobody had said anything – nobody had spoken – but little Mika had been sure, more certain than he had ever felt of anything, that his dad was not taking them back to mama and their chalet, but abducting them. He couldn't have said why he'd felt that or how it made any sense. He'd just been sure, and terrified. He had thought about opening the car door and throwing his small body from the car, like the true George Michael would do many years later, travelling down a motorway, but he was too worried about abandoning Di, about something bad happening to her. Then the wheels of the car had swerved into the turning that led to the great multicoloured gates of the holiday park. There were the sand dunes. There was the salty sea air. The car came to a halt, and he watched as his dad put his hand on Di's bare thigh – she was wearing a miniskirt – and left it there. As if (he felt his heart hurt, now, at the hard heavy irony) to reassure her.

The count went down. Seven. Six. Five.

Was that what a man was. Was that what he, little Mika, would grow up to be?

No. He never would.

The count went down. Four. Three.

He knew and he didn't know why Di had collapsed, become ill, risen from her bedridden state and left, only then to succumb to the booze. He knew and he didn't know, he thought, what had happened and that what had happened had something, everything, nothing—

>—'*Hey,*' Fin says again because Daniel's expression is alarming – Daniel's face is scrunched and immobile: —

—everything
to do with his dad, who wasn't Di's dad, who was dead now, whom Mika had let die.

Funny, he thought, what a life is.

The count was down to two, then one.

He thought again of his kid, his kid called—*

---

* '*Woah...*'

†

The world winks—

‡

§

---
† 'What the fuck?'
‡ 'Hi Daniel.'
§ '*Huh?*'

¶

[rocks rumble and move]

**

The world w-w-winks—

[the ground is collapsing]

††

‡‡

§§

[the last 'a' of Daniel's name tumbles too]

¶   'Hi Daniel, it's Crystal.'
** 'But it can't be—'
†† 'It is though. It's me – Crystal.'
‡‡ 'But....but Crystal never called me Daniel.'
§§ 'Exactly!'

¶¶

***

[the ground is collapsing] [salt shakes ~~from the ceiling~~]

The world w-w-w-winks—

[the last 'a' of Daniel's name gets crushed by cascading salt pillars]

[collapsing]

†††

‡‡‡

§§§

[pop! goes another rubbery pink bubble]

¶¶ 'I…*ugh*…'
*** 'It's OK. I know you're still pissed off with me.'
††† '…*ummm*….Huh?'
‡‡‡ 'I know you still think I should never have dumped that settee. I know a part of you believes I left you just like your mum did, but I didn't – not completely. It's a long time since I first came here, to where you are right now. What was Fin's name for it? Yeah, *Never Was*. It was different back then. It had nothing of you in it then. It wasn't even you I was meant to lead here, kidda, but I knew, almost as soon as I met you – and after you told me your theory of the Universe, definitely – that you'd end up coming too, eventually.'
§§§ 'I….*ummm*….'

¶¶¶

****

[salt shakes] [the ground is collapsing]

The world w-w-w-winks—

††††

‡‡‡‡

[collapsing] [collapsing]

[Crystal's turquoise-jewelled earrings crash through time and space]

[the settee crashes too] [coins fly from its crevices]

¶¶¶ 'What Fin says is true, by the way. This place isn't really a place at all. It's like I imagine the bottom of the flash being, littered with trash and shitty little nothings, bottle top grips, throwaway whims and – *hmmmm* – antique condoms. Half thoughts that got snagged on somebody's tongue and then ended up snagging them in turn. Maybe by now you've figured it by out, or maybe you haven't. You always were kind of stubborn, Daniel.'

**** 'I....*ummm*....Crystal?

†††† '*Yesssss* kidda, it really is me, or it's the bits of me that are stuck here. What Fin's trying to tell you about being able to leave – that's true too, mostly. Once you've left you're not meant to return. Everybody has their own version of *Never Was* and everybody has their own interpretation of it, but nobody's supposed to keep coming back over and over, like I did. Like I'm still doing. No matter what happened, no matter how much time passed, I kept getting drawn back to *Never Was*, like a junky. Like you turned out to be! Yeah, I know – I know all about that part of you, Daniel.'

‡‡‡‡ 'But....*ugh*....how could Crystal...how could you possibly know that about me? We haven't seen each other or spoken in years, because you left not long after the—'

§§§§
¶¶¶¶
*****

[but where have Daniel's sunglasses gone?] [pop!]

The world w-w-w-winks—

†††††

‡‡‡‡‡

[collapsing!]

§§§§§

---

§§§§ 'Woah, steady there kidda. Don't get me wrong, you've definitely made progress. Finally – finally! – you've allowed yourself to see that it was Mika, not me, who caused the collapses...or it was all that wild brine pumping or some invisible brine run that suddenly flooded or it was corporate neglect or it was all of those things plus Mika's stumbling, fussing distraction. But who was distracting him, Daniel? Who kept on interrupting his thoughts? Who swerved his attention and sent it to-ing and fro-ing? Who was it who ultimately caused the – what was it you said the collapses ended up being called?'
¶¶¶¶ 'The....*er*.....Great Subsidence? But – but I wasn't interrupting Mika's thoughts *then*. I wasn't actually there at the time. I was just—'
***** 'What?'
††††† 'I....*ugh*....'
‡‡‡‡‡ 'I know you understand more than you're letting on, Daniel. It's like you're realizing so much it's really scrambling your mind, right? Or maybe realizing is the wrong word for it. I remember the feeling – it's like doing one of those Magic Eye puzzles. But how do I know you turned out a drug addict? High functioning, sure, but hopelessly addicted? Because here I can *feeeeel* it. I can feel whatever you've taken overtaking you right now, because some of me is still suspended in *Never Was* too, because I couldn't do what Fin's trying to do – leave, and let *Never Was* take that weightless weight from me. Think about it. I told you I'd prove I was murderer.'
§§§§§ 'I....*ugh*....I don't understand....Is *Never Was* true? Is this...is here..... *hhhhmm*.....the future?

¶¶¶¶¶

******

††††††

######

[there's no difference, now, between ceiling and ground]

The world w-w-w-winks—

[collapsing!] [collapsing!]

¶¶¶¶¶ 'Oh my fucking god, kidda. I'm *trying* to help you, just like Fin is. You always knew I didn't really kill anybody. You've always been stubborn but you've never been stupid. Sat in that McDonald's chomping your Filet O'Fish and watching me suck my McNuggets to death, you knew, right from the very beginning, that I hadn't killed anybody. But you wanted to know why I would say such a thing, and you wanted to know because you'd already felt the answer in your own skinny ribs – you just didn't have the words for it. But now you do. Or at least, now you have a way of narrating it, or whatever, because in my version of *Never Was* I was everything I ever said I was. By this point, I'm a fucking serial killer. It's exhausting!'

****** But Crystal, that's completely crazy. I....How could you—?'

†††††† 'As crazy as following Fin around and telling Fin your life story without even knowing who Fin is? As crazy as a wrecked cruise ship recovering? As unbelievable? You see, just like Fin has always been famous in *Never Was*, here I've always been what nobody would ever bother to think of me, and it'll be the same with you when Fin leaves. Or OK, it'll be similar. Who knows what your version of *Never Was* will be like? You've already begun to see the way things work here, unpredictably and without consistency – a bit like Mika!'

‡‡‡‡‡‡ 'But...*ummmmm*.....Mika's not here....Mika's dead....Or no, not yet, Mika's trapped underground in the mine, because of the.....the explosion. The accident all those years ago. The explosion of the explosion. The cause of the Great Subsidence and—'

§§§§§
⁋⁋⁋⁋⁋
****

[the last 'a' of Daniel's name is lost to the world]

††††††
‡‡‡‡‡‡

The world w-w-w-winks—

[but so too is the world lost to Daniel]

§§§§§§

[pop!][collapsing!]

⁋⁋⁋⁋⁋⁋

---

§§§§§ 'And Mika will survive the crush – just about – and you'll grow up and grow tits – just like I said – and do well at school – kidda, who *knew* – and then, when you're as far away as you could possibly be, a world away from that house by the side of the wide road, he'll die. You know how that story turns out. And you know – I know you do – that you abandoned me just as much as I abandoned you. That's what people *do*, kidda. They throw away other people so they can throw away a part of themselves. Well, where do you think that part of them goes?'
⁋⁋⁋⁋⁋ '....*um*...I....I'm confused...I—.'
******* 'Keep resisting if it makes you feel better. What difference does it make? You're here in *Never Was* either way. But listen, Daniel. This is important. Try as hard as you like, you won't find a single reason for why I was the way I was – or think of it this way, all the reasons lead here, to *Never Was*. I know people thought I was damaged goods. I know you thought that I just needed love, just like yourself, but unlike you I wasn't bothered by my mum dying – and we all know your mum might as well have died, kidda. You hated everything because of her going, but when my mum died, I loved it, because it gave me a reason to be as furious as I already was. I—'
†††††† 'I know…I know what you're going to say. You're going to say that you wished for it.'
‡‡‡‡‡‡ 'No, I wished the *world* would die. When I told you that lie about pouring bleach into my eye—'
§§§§§§ 'But it wasn't a lie. It was a metaphor. A way of explaining something to me that you couldn't have said any other way—'
⁋⁋⁋⁋⁋⁋ '*Huh*. I guess so. I made up a hundred different explanations. I said all *sorts* of things. Maybe in the end you were relieved to be rid of me – maybe

****

[the gone ground gives way to the metallic walls of a toilet cubicle]

[a mirrored cuboid – a mini hall of mirrors]

††††††††

The world w-w-w-winks—

‡‡‡‡‡‡‡‡

[the silver walls reflect a distorted body]

§§§§§§§§

[twisting limbs and a broken torso]

[the cubicle is in a club somewhere]

---

that's why you've never tried to try and contact me since. But imagine if I hadn't ever turned up at your house, kidda! You'd never have got hold of my sunglasses and you'd never have attempted to teleport yourself out of your karaoke version of reality by deciding to believe you should have been famous. Not that you already *were* famous, like your friend Fin here. No – that you should have been famous but never would be. Both vain and desolate at the same time, huh? But then – that's also why you're here now. That, and whatever it is that the fame is an alibi for.'
******** 'I.....ugh....but.....*errrrummmmmm*......Whadoyoumean, an *alibi*?'
†††††††† 'Woah, kidda, you don't seem too good. Blood's thudding from your nose. Are those tears too? What is it you need – speed? Amphetamines? Pepsi?'
‡‡‡‡‡‡‡‡ '.....*errrrummmmmm*.......ugh.......?'
§§§§§§§§ 'Yikes. Looks like this time you've taken too much. I'm sorry. I'm really sorry. It's about time I was going anyway. You don't want to risk getting caught up in my *Never Was*, trust me. Have you ever heard of the word *neonaticide*? It's when you murder your own child within the first twenty-four hours of its life. You do realise, don't you, kidda, that you shouldn't even be able to hear me? Fin is your designated guide, your – what's it called – *listener* – so really I should...really I...—'

[inside the cubicle crouches Daniel]   [pop!]

The world w-w-w-winks—

[whose bent body it is that is being distorted]

¶¶¶¶¶¶¶

[who is simultaneously still sat beside Fin on a cliff edge]

¶¶¶¶¶¶¶ '...*ughh*...my what? *Huh? Eruummmmm*.....Crystal? How could you...? Erummmmm....Wh-where are you? Crystal?'

III

...Crystal?—

—'Phew!' Fin exclaims, hearing Daniel at last speak again. 'I thought I'd lost you.'

I...*ummm?*—

—Fin has been slapping Daniel's sweat-slicked face for a minute or more now. Daniel is sweating profusely. Where Fin and Daniel are – wherever *Never Was* is – the weather has suddenly worsened. The swirly sky has turned angry and fierce, as if a blizzard has combined with a solar storm. The winged creature Daniel once thought was a gull yelps as it leaps out of the path of speeding clouds; cumulo clouds that once were puffy and fluffed have become heavy rolling masses, more like boulders. The junky waves are now wildly gesticulating. The cruise ship holds her own within them, though; she's so much sturdier, now, than she once was.

Daniel gasps.
Daniel gasps.
Daniel gasps.

I – I've lost—

    —'It's OK,' croaks Fin, above the weather's din. 'I was just saying I thought I'd lost you. You were out for the count!'
    'No,' says Daniel, gasping again. The blizzard-cum-solar-storm swells, retracts, swells again. 'No – I'm somewhere else. I'm somewhere else and I – I...'

I've lost my sunglasses and become convinced that the world, itself, has stolen them. The world is staring back at me from behind their blue tint, and because of this, I cannot trust the world. I can't tell what the world is thinking but—

> —Where Fin and Daniel are, the weather is already settling again. But as it settles everything simultaneously seems more changed, or more changing, than ever. The cruise ship has almost completely recovered, arisen from her bedridden state again. The creature hovering above the ship looks unquestionably like a pterosaur. The snow on the ground melts, returns, melts again. The flower Fin gave Daniel earlier has lost all but one of its petals now – it's not dead, but it's not recognisable anymore. Were Daniel to look back down the cliff, sideways, away from the sea-view, Daniel would see that Fin's mansion, too, is now mutating in form. At the moment it looks something like a cross between a McDonald's and the kind of bulky out-of-town building that might home a SnowDome; either that, or it's a warehouse-style club, the kind that soundwaves pulsate from. Its sides are marked out with a ribbon of blue neon.

Daniel gasps.
Now it's Fin turn to hiccup.
'I don't think the world *thinks* anything,' Fin says, after hiccupping.

But that's what it feels like. That's the only way I can begin to describe the way that it feels. I keep catching bits and pieces of the world, snatches of sound, snaggles of colour, but then when I try to connect what I've caught to a cause, I can't, because the world is expressionless. It's saying things and making manic gestures, but I can't tell what it means by anything.—

—'I think,' says Fin, whose eyelids are slowly beginning to droop; either the afterparty has finally caught up with Fin, or the changeable weather has made Fin feel sleepy. Change can do that. 'I think,' Fin begins again, resisting the oncoming sleepiness, 'that this is the bit when you remember where you were right before here, where you were immediately before you ended up in *Never Was* – where you were before you turned up at my afterparty. I remember – I remember how it was for me. I remember being in that changing room I told you about, telling Miss Universe about the state I was in, the sorry state I was in, before I myself wound up in *Never Was*.'

Fin hiccups again.

Fin's eyelids struggle not to slump. It's a funny combination, hiccups and sleepiness.

Daniel, however, is oblivious.

I thought I heard Crystal speak, but now I'm not so sure. I'm not sure if I was just imagining her voice, whether she was there, or here, or anywhere. I can't tell what the world means by a thing, because the world is wearing my sunglasses.—

— 'So?' Fin yawns.

So I'm trying to get them back. Just a few moments ago – it could easily have been hours – I snatched out for their frames in front of me, but the movement was difficult and threw me back on my heels, and my bum cascaded backwards. Many versions of my bum; a multitude of my bums. The world let out a low half-laugh, which went on for hours, much longer than it felt like I fell for. Then something caught hold of my hand, or my hand caught hold of something; I couldn't tell what was meant by the hard protrusion my slippery fingers had caught hold of, but at least I didn't fall into the—

—'Toilet', says Fin. 'You're in a—'

I'm in a K-hole.—

—'That too,' Fin agrees, sleepier and sleepier.

I'm in the dead space of a—

> —'K-hole,' Fin repeats, very wearily. 'You might have to explain what that is though.'

For one hot second, I have clarity.—

> —Fin, meanwhile, has fallen fast asleep, head at rest on Daniel's shoulder, already dribbling a bit.
>
> Daniel continues anyway, as if in a trance, as if everything depends on what is next to come.

I know exactly where I am and where I have been before now. I'm in the dead space of K-hole.

I've taken too much ketamine, one too many white powdery lines. I was riding the wonky bounce of it fine; the world was lopsided but lucid; I knew what it meant when the ground met my step and my body touched hard surfaces expectantly, knowing which edges were soft and which were not, even if they felt soft. But then I became greedy. I wanted the bounce to be bigger and bigger. I wanted more, so I took more, and then – just like that – the world was gone and obscure, because the world was wearing my sunglasses.

Just a couple of hours earlier, I was waiting in line outside the club. The ground there was mushy with slush, everywhere puckered with unburied litter. It was early morning and the sun was fuzzy and reluctant. I was rolling a cigarette but didn't have a filter, so I tapped the shoulder of somebody in front of me. The queue for the club was bitterly long, hushed but nervy. Snow was struggling to land on my shoulders. In front of me, a hundred or so bodies beyond, was the club's entrance, where the bouncers stood rubbing their palms in their palms, sometimes nodding, sometimes not nodding.

When they nodded a body dipped into the dim of the building's interior. When they didn't nod, somebody was disappointed.

It made me think of a scene in the film of *The Neverending Story*, when Atreyu the boy-hero is struggling to save the decaying land of Fantasia and on his way to the Southern Oracle to learn how to do so, but first he has to pass through something called the 'mirror gate', a kind of portal. Engywook, a research scientist gnome, warns that the mirror is where people encounter their true form: kind people find that they are cruel, and brave men discover they're cowards.

In the scene, Atreyu slowly approaches the mirror, which is wedged in thick snow and held tight by icicles, and sees in its reflection the face of Bastian, the real-world boy who has been reading the story of Atreyu's quest, his attempt to save Fantasia from the Nothing.

I hadn't particularly wanted to go out, but I hadn't particularly not wanted to either. It was the time of my life when I was in the habit of going out all the time, and even if I didn't feel like partying, burying my body and mind in the Nothing was preferable to passing through the day's ordinariness. Or maybe ordinariness was the Nothing. Ordinariness was after all a kind of cruelty; that's what I had come to think anyway. For a day to be ordinary it had to have recognisable contours: everyday objects were fated to their fixed form; the kettle had to keep to its shape; the solitary moon had to stay suspended in space, and not fall through the floor of the universe – like its long lost sibling had done centuries ago, when I was younger.

Plus all the little *things* that made a day pass dependably themselves depended on somebody else's labour, or even impoverishment, and in that sense ordinariness was a kind of theft. My world was the unmaking of others' worlds, and I wanted none of it.

By this point in my life, Mika had died – from lung cancer caused by salt inhalation or a million skinny rollies – but I made a good living and was doing OK, lived abroad, far away from the North. I was doing OK, but I wanted the Nothing.

I wanted the Nothing, whatever it was.

While I'd been stood in the queue for the club, a dog walker had approached the line frowning. His dog wobbled beside him, its ears grotty, its nose to the ground sniffling for other dogs' shit, sometimes glancing up at its owner. It seemed to me to want to move on. But the man stood still, staring. Then he began to shout at all the club-kids in the line, telling us that we were selfish and ignorant. Other people were suffering, he screamed. The world was dying, he said, and all we could do was queue for a party.

The man was a white man, maybe middle-aged. He was white as a sheet by the time he finished screaming; white as I would be when, a few hours later, I overdid it and fell into the K-Hole. The walker wandered off eventually, kicking a beer can into the sorry fuzz of the morning. It was the time of my life when I went out in the mornings, to parties that never stopped and never began. His dog looked, I thought, embarrassed.

In another scene in *The Neverending Story*, a group of characters, all inhabitants of Fantasia, discuss the Nothing. What it is, and where it comes from. One of the characters speaks of Fantasia's North, where the Nothing is fast encroaching. He struggles to account for the force of it – the cause of it, as well as its destructive effects. He talks of a lake that just suddenly disappeared. 'It wasn't there anymore; nothing was there anymore,' he says. When another character asks if what was left was a hole, he replies 'No,' because 'a hole would have been something.'

The Nothing is not something. The Nothing is what's left when there's no longer something. Or maybe the Nothing is what's always there waiting, waiting for the feeling of there being something to subside.

For a while as a kid, I'd watched the film of *The Neverending Story* endlessly, on repeat, but when my mum left I'd mostly forgotten about it. Beneath the blanket of Mika's silences, I came to prefer the soap opera realities of *Neighbours* and *Home & Away* to the sad blasted landscapes of Fantasia. Instead of attaching my fantasies to characters without reality – fantastic warriors like Atreyu, with his long hair – I became fascinated instead by characters who inhabited a reality that was closer to mine, but which was, at the same time, far away, the other side of the still-turning globe, like and unlike mine.

It was the difference between a world that could have been true, but was not, and a world that could never have been true – a world that never was, even before the Nothing came for it.

By the time of the time in the toilet – by the time the world wore my sunglasses – I was in my mid-twenties. I was neither Atreyu nor Bastian nor Henry Ramsay from *Neighbours*, but somewhere on the other side of fantasy's other side. My body had grown in the way Crystal had predicted; my body had grown breasts and I regretted it. Regret is a strange and difficult thing to feel for your body. How can you regret something you didn't do? How can something that is irrevocably you come to feel, nonetheless, regrettable?

It seems impossible, but it's possible. I could call it grief instead – I could say I felt grief for the body my body was not, the body my body once seemed like it might have become, but which, by now, was long lost. Now my body was marked and I was called names because of it – girl, woman, *her*. Each of those words felt like names to me, but my body invited them.

Each of those words settled on other people's tongues, like snow, when they saw me.

But the same snow would not fall on me.

Whenever I expressed distaste for my form – whenever I complained about the shape of my chest – friends, men usually but women too, would rebuff me with something I understood as a panicked pragmatism. 'Well, you have them at the end of the day,' they'd say, or 'How do you think I feel about having a penis?' Fair enough, I thought, but sometimes what's necessary is a reckoning with unmaterialised loss, a way of dealing with the loss of what never was.

If you can't touch the Nothing – if you can't get close to it – it'll only consume you. Everybody knows that, one way or another.

By the time the world wore my sunglasses – by the time of the time in the toilet – I was doing OK, but I was also a junky. I consumed excessively. Sometimes every day, from first thing in the morning onwards, to the extent that excess was my ordinary.

It was a long time since I'd left home and moved abroad, and a long time, too, since I'd thought about Crystal. Mika had only recently died, but in the years before he did, I'd hardly phoned him, and in that sense his death hadn't mattered much. I resented the time I'd spent by his bedside when I was still a kid, after the Great Subsidence. The explosion in the mine had left him immobilized at first, and for a while he'd had to use a wheelchair, a fate that he had taken badly, though the doctors had assured him he'd walk again. For a month or so I had nursed him in bed like he had nursed his half-sister, Di, many years ago – in another pebbledashed house by the side of the wide road, Mika told me. I'd never known, before then, very much about Di. I had never known Mika to speak so much about his own life.

He didn't for long. His intimacy lasted as long as he was bedridden, strewn like a helpless babba on the bedsheets, crushed into the pillows and surrounded by fragments of trash, chocolate bar wrappers and neon-coloured fizzy lollipops. He only wanted to eat sickly sweet things for a while. He wouldn't touch anything that tasted of salt, anything that was mildly salted. I would smuggle in small bags of McDonald's fries and lick my greased fingers secretly, while Mika deliriously mumbled.

Sometimes he spoke softly, sometimes severely. 'Why do you wear those sunglasses all the time, Daniela?' he said once, his eyelashes thick with sleep now, not salt, the skin of his lips dry, and fraying.

But I wasn't wearing sunglasses by Mika's bedside – I'd put them down like a child's toy the day of the explosion, the explosion of the explosion, or whatever it was that caused the collapses. It had taken them three days to extract the workers, three days to mine the live bodies of the miners. Meanwhile lines of subsidence spread through the town like never before, sinking strips of ground, ripping up the patio that Mika had built in our front yard, tipping our house slightly, tilting it.

It was as if the Nothing had returned with full force – it was as if, having turned my back on Fantasia, the Nothing turned on me in turn. That was what it felt like.

A limbo for lost dreams and things that never came to be

What makes something – anything – difficult to believe? Or just difficult to see? Believability is a funny thing. Some live within its bounds constantly. Some people believe, without any doubt, that the ground is right there beneath their feet. Wealth helps – if you have wealth, a steady income, you have a stable background and you have consistency; the world comes to seem increasingly trustworthy, and this repeated consistency in turn frees you to believe in the reality of what is within you – in its ordinariness, as well as its significance.

Wealth helps, except when it doesn't. Just like ordinariness, interiority is always precarious. That's why, in fiction, it comes naturally to some characters, others less so.

When Mika was bedridden and uncharacteristically communicative, it seemed surreal, even when he made sense. I wasn't used to him speaking intimately, and I wasn't used to thinking he thought about the past, and I definitely wasn't used to his moments of tenderness, which alternated with outbursts of stifled aggression, an aggression his wrecked body could neither hold nor communicate. It felt awkward, embarrassing, even obscene, listening to his need to be listened to. Names popped from his mouth uncontrollably, like hiccups: the name of my mum, the name of his mum, Diana/Di, even Ace, never Crystal. I kept wondering if he thought my hovering body belonged to each of the names that he called – whether he was hallucinating, or whether he was just calling out for somebody, everybody, who wasn't there anymore. Once, hilariously, he kept asking for himself. Or he kept saying his full name in the form of a question – 'George Michael? George Michael?'

Then his hand scuttled, crablike, across the bedding, towards a half-eaten chocolate bar. He couldn't quite reach it, I realised, but for a while I let his fingers struggle for it – for a while, but not long enough for him to accuse me of cruelty, I was cruel to him.

Eventually I would come to learn how to use that discrepancy between what was inside me and what people expected of me – between my intentions and what people made of me – to my advantage. What people expected of me had to do with the way they read the contours of my body, and the names they called me because of it. But my body was not mine, and I was not aligned with the thoughts and desires they expected to find inside it, and because of this, I could trick and tease. I could shift the ground beneath people's feet.

Or so I thought. For a while I cleaved to this discrepancy as if it was my only weapon in the world. For that, I thank and blame Crystal.

By the time of the time in the toilet cubicle – by the time I fell into this K-hole – I had taken again to wearing sunglasses inside. To hide the hard glaze of my eyes, mostly. Not long before the world took them from me, I had been sat at a bar in the club alone, on a high stool. I wasn't ready to dance, wasn't high enough. A man came over and sat down on a stool beside me. He was wearing, of all things, a cowboy hat. By this point in my life I had sex mostly with women, but when cowboy man said, without saying anything else, that he wanted to fuck me, I just said 'OK then'.

We went down to a place in the club's basement, to a corner that was both private and not private.

My response was instant and unthinking, but when I thought about it, I thought I hadn't want to give him the gift of resistance – I thought that by denying him the need to convince me, the need to seduce me, I had beaten him. I thought I had trumped him by making it easy for him – I thought I had shifted the ground beneath his feet, feminized *him*, silently taken his conquest away from him.

I felt nothing – no pleasure and no pain – but feeling nothing only made me feel closer to the body my body was not. Feeling nothing made my body remember the body my body had forgotten, and not forgotten. It was like a magic trick. By surrendering, I made myself elsewhere. Throughout the whole thing, I kept my sunglasses on.

The story sounds like a bad joke when I tell it. 'A man in a cowboy hat walks into a bar...'

Later on, while I was still just about sober, still knowing a surface when I touched it, cowboy man came up to me again, and asked me my name.

'Daniel,' I almost said, but then didn't.

Nor did I ask him his name.

In my head – who knows why it came to me then – was the memory of Crystal's visit, her crimped fringe, her socks shoved into her high red heels, her *Luckys* and bubbles and cold unfathomable claim about killing somebody, about being a murderer. I'd never known for sure what she'd meant by that. Nor of course had I ever proved to her there were two moons – my world's second moon had never shown its face, just as Crystal's first murder hadn't left any evidence, any trace, any indication of ever having taken place. Then the moon fell through the floor of the universe anyway. Then the floor of the universe fell through itself.

I had never understood what Crystal meant when she'd insisted she was a murderer, but now, having almost told cowboy man my true name, I nearly understood. I came closer to *Never Was*.

'Who do you think *you* are anyway?' cowboy man said, before walking away, away to the deep throb of the dancefloor.

Crystal left not long after the collapses, not long after Mika's explosives overblew, sending shivers through our town, trapping the miners underground. My memory of those days was always hazy at best, and Mika's refusal to acknowledge Crystal's presence in our house had confused me. His refusal confused me so much that her visit quickly came to seem to me like a cruel dream, which was perhaps what it had always been to Mika. I realised that while I sat by his bedside, listening to his broken stories of Di, his half-sister not the Princess, and seeing the brittle fondness in his eyes, a fondness that seemed to break on him like waves – like the waves of a sea slushy with junk.

Caring for Mika matured me. Or perhaps it just so happened that I hit puberty – or puberty violently hit me – during the time I tended to his body by his bedside. Maybe it was all just a coincidence. But it was time consuming and I quickly saw that it – caring for Mika, and simultaneously hating him – could easily consume me. I became disciplined. I started going regularly to school, whose building has survived the ripples of subsidence that surged through our town after the explosion. There it stood, sturdy and unfazed, unbothered by the world's cracked surface. I came to like entering its gates.

One day I went home at lunchtime to bring Mika his food while he was still bedridden, before they brought him the wheelchair. I stepped over the ruptured remains of his patio, slid into the hallway, onto the scuffed lino tiles of our kitchen. There, perched on the kitchen table gathering dust, were my sunglasses, which once had been Crystal's.

I don't know why I hadn't noticed them before – I don't know why I hadn't put them away, in a drawer, the day I put them down. But in any case, I saw them then for what they were, which was just a way of signalling I wasn't there.

For a while at least, the shock of the collapses snapped me out that feeling – or maybe it was Crystal's departure that did the trick. With her, or with the going ground, had gone the final 'a' of my name, but I hadn't told anybody. But I think that it was around then, when I saw the dusty frames sat on the table, that I grasped the meaning of the feeling that had attached to their worn frames, the feeling that was still in me despite no longer wearing them – the feeling that I should have been famous, but would not be.

Fame is always in some ways a metaphor – a metaphor for the way a life falls away from itself, becomes something other than what it once might have been, splits, shivers, is briefly felt, like the presence of a ghost, by somebody somewhere else, before they realize it was only a breeze – a breeze blowing in nothing. But fame is also a form of recognition, a song hummed and instantly known.

It wasn't that I wanted to be famous – not really. It was just that I felt a queer and difficult affinity with the feeling of not having become what I should have been. Even before I didn't become what I could have been, I felt that affinity, I mean. A synonym for fame is sometimes *making it* – being OK, and not succumbing.

The lives of the legendary are very disposable. That's why we love them.

Mika loved Princess Di – or at least, if he didn't love her life or even really know much about it, then he loved the delicate figure of her, the look of her in the form of an easily breakable mermaid, her fishy skirts susceptible to the tumble of cigarette ash, welcoming it.

Susceptibility is another funny thing. Which of my tendencies will come to be? Which of my susceptibilities will I have the means to outlive? Which will I swim silently by, unaware of how close I came to them? Where do they come from? Can I swim or not?

She – Princess Diana's namesake, Di, Crystal's mum, Mika's half-sister – had stopped and started at life, or her life had stopped and started, started and stopped, then fallen away from itself. Mika said, when he was deliriously bedridden, that he regretted not helping her. He told me to tell her he was sorry. When I said I couldn't tell her because she was dead, he looked at me like I was crazy. He himself had seen her in this very house just the other day. 'Can you even see *anything* in those sunglasses?' he said to me.

But I wasn't wearing my shades by Mika's bedside.

But at the same time, I understood. But what I understood was brittle and barely there, because what I knew then without being able to say was that Mika had seen his half-sister in Crystal, and because of this, he couldn't see Crystal – couldn't hear the hum of her version of femininity as she slipped through our rooms, couldn't recognise her, couldn't bear to.

Or maybe that's just what I wanted to believe I'd understood. Maybe Mika's cruelty to Crystal was without cause – maybe Mika's cruelty was just general. The Nothing comes for us softly, severely.

As soon as I could, I left the disturbed contours of our town, the jilted McDonald's and disrupted roads, and went out into a world that was ruinous. The weather worsened and worsened. The seasons became increasingly unrecognisable. I never attempted to get in touch with Crystal. I never worried, not much, how Mika was doing. I just worried about myself mostly. I often thought about walking out on my life, but then I'd think that I'd already done that. I went to parties. By the time of my mid-twenties gender was less of a destiny, the Internet was changing everything, but I was oblivious. The drugs I danced to sank into the rest of my life, saddened my saddening eyes, and I took to wearing sunglasses inside again – I took to wearing them everywhere again, as if I was somebody. I sometimes compared my life to an unplayable video game, a game I didn't have the necessary gear for, or a game meant for a machine that had always been obsolescent.

My life was not precious to me, but I was precious about *it*, definitely.—

>—As Daniel pauses, Fin starts stirring. The sun of *Never Was* is setting. The sky is calm now. Snow gently tumbles. Out at sea, the waves tip and tinkle and occasionally simmer. The funnel of the cruise ship whistles sweetly.

But something Crystal said to me just before she left always stayed with me.—

>—'Hhhhm?' Fin says, waking. Fin's time in *Never Was* is nearly done now. 'What was that?' Fin asks, prodding Daniel's ribs. 'What were you saying? Did I miss something?'

She was stood in my bedroom packing her suitcase. The white band with fluorescent green stripes was still tied to the case's handle. Crystal's fringe was still crimped and while watching her pack, I saw for the first time the corded device that she used to forge the crinkles. She told me she was going to live with her actual dad, who lived in the South by an actual sea, not some dumb underground sea that didn't exist but which had still managed to rip everything up anyhow. She also said her dad was a millionaire. I nodded quietly. Crystal sounded younger, then, than I'd ever heard her sound. Without removing her eyes from the blouse she was folding, she told me I could keep her sunglasses. 'Thanks,' I said, even though by then I'd taken them off. 'You know, kidda,' she said, closing her flowery suitcase, zipping it shut, 'The thing with you is that you want to disappear, but you also want everybody to *watch* – you want the whole fucking world to watch you disappear.' Then she lit the last *Lucky* I ever saw her smoke. 'That makes you totally obnoxious,' she said, and then, in a different tone, 'but it's also what will keep you afloat, whenever the time comes.'—

> —'See,' says Fin, rubbing away sleep. 'In her own way, Crystal was telling you about this place – about *Never Was*.'

She also declared that Ace was queer – somehow she'd known I was wondering why she wasn't saying goodbye to him – and that it never would have worked out between them anyway. Mika would have made it impossible, she said. 'Your dad's racist,' she said, cupping her elbow in her free hand as she smoked that last *Lucky*. It was a pose she had copied from somewhere – it was how film stars stood when they smoked, I thought. 'You *do* know that,' Crystal added, between short sharp drags, absently tapping her ash on my duvet, 'don't you?'—

—'Did you?' Fin asks.

'I guess I knew and didn't know,' Daniel replies, 'just like I knew and didn't know about Mika's dressing.'

'I don't think the two things are really comparable,' Fin says.

'No,' says Daniel, a little put out. 'I didn't mean that. Of course I didn't.'

Both Fin and Daniel stare out to sea. The cruise ship has now completely recovered; she sits proud and resplendent atop the junky waves. On her bow is an oval swimming pool. On her aft, just about visible from the clifftop, is something that looks like it might be a helipad.

'Maybe that's exactly the problem,' Fin says, after a bit. 'The fact that you could know without knowing that Mika was racist, or that he might have been. Maybe that's what whiteness is in a way, the privilege of knowing without knowing.'

'I'm not sure I understand what you mean,' Daniel says.

Fin says nothing in reply. A snowflake touches the end of Daniel's nose; this time Fin brushes it off.

'I'm *cold*,' Daniel complains, suddenly shivering.

'It's just the drugs,' Fin shrugs. 'Part of you is still in that toilet cubicle drenched in the melting dimensions of your K-Hole. Some of you is here, but some of you is still there.'

Fin pauses.

'And it'll stay that way until you leave *Never Was*. Until you leave your *Never Was*, I mean.'

'My version?'

'Yes.'

The funnel of the cruise ship lets out a great puff of smoke. The feathered creature Fin is convinced is a pterosaur circles the smoke, sniffs at it. Then the creature lands, deftly and with grace, on the ship's helipad.

A beat passes.

'So all this,' Daniel says, waving a weary arm, '*is* yours after all? Everything here is a materialisation of your disappointments and throwaway thoughts, your sunken dreams and faltering desires?'

'Almost,' Fin replies, clearly a little exasperated, by this point. 'I asked you if you wanted to be in my future memoir, didn't I?'

'Sure, though I'm not sure I know what the word *future* means anymore.'

'That's because *Never Was* is just the future's indeterminacy,' Fin says, as if it's the most obvious thing in the world. 'It's full of futures that never were, but being here brings you closer to something in you that might otherwise have died – something that might have petered out, like the lines of a half-remembered jingle or song. Your time in *Never Was* is far from over, but already it's having an effect on you. Like I was trying to tell you before, some of this landscape has become yours since you arrived here, at my afterparty, and some of it is leftover from those who were here before either of us – Miss Universe, who I told you about, and who knows how many others.'

'Crystal?'

Fin looks hard at Daniel. 'You yourself said you thought you heard her voice.'

'But she's not *here* in any meaningful sense of the word. Is she?'

'Maybe not, but I have a sense of her. I've never actually met her, here or anywhere, but I have a sense of her. I told you I could see her in you.'

'And I told you I hated stories,' says Daniel, still grumpy, changing the subject.

'That's true,' Fin says.

'I hate it when you say that.'

The two figures on the cliff edge go quiet again. The flower Fin passed Daniel earlier has now utterly wilted. Its last shrivelled petal is faintly multicoloured. Daniel presses the limp umbel into the snow. Out at sea, the cruise ship shakes off the last of the junk crusted to her sides. For the first time in a long time, Daniel looks back down the cliff. The light is dim – the sun's almost down – but it's still possible to see that the sea has now swallowed the Ha Ha. The terrace of Fin's mansion is as dishevelled as Mika's patio. It's as if time has shifted but neither forwards or backwards – it's as if time in *Never Was* is like the tide, sometimes encroaching, sometimes receding.

'I still don't know who you are,' Daniel says, turning back again, now, to look at Fin. 'You still haven't told me *your* story. How you came to be here. Who you *really* are.'

Fin sighs. 'But I told you something. As a child I used to believe I was famous – I believed I was famous and I behaved that way. What more do you think you need to know? That I had a fan club with no members? That I wrote lyrics for songs with no music? That I was always waiting for my helicopter to arrive, always expecting it to be there waiting for me when I came out of school? That I wrote autographs on little torn pieces of paper, and left them for strangers on benches in bus shelters? Or shall I tell you some other story – shall I tell you I imagined I was the reincarnation of an ancient Greek hero? Out of time, unseasonable?'

Fin pauses, as if waiting for a laugh. Daniel waits, unlaughing.

'Or would it help if I told you I loved pterosaurs?' Fin says, eyes fixed on the creature sitting on the ship's helipad.

'OK,' says Daniel, following Fin's gaze. 'Fine. But you haven't said why. You haven't said *why* you believed you were famous, what it was that made you – I don't know, *dissociate* like that. You haven't gone into detail or told me the reasons – and that means you haven't really told me anything.'

'I think you already know what you need to know about me,' Fin says, very quietly now. 'Either that, or it doesn't matter.'

Daniel's amber eyes show disappointment.

Fin notices.

'You know, the flowers of birdsfoot trefoil actually have five petals, not three.'

'What's *that* got to do with anything?'

'During all of the time you've been by my side,' Fin says, slowly, patiently, 'have you ever wondered whether I was boy or a girl, a man or a woman? Have you ever wondered what pronoun to use for me?'

This question takes Daniel back a bit.

'No. I – I guess I haven't actually thought about it.'

'Well, there you go,' and then, almost as an afterthought, one not necessarily spoken for Daniel's ears, 'Perhaps that's what my Ha Ha was all about. I've been wondering.'

'*Huh?*'

Fin stands up, stretches, brushes off some snow. Daniel stays seated.

'Listen, I've already told you my theory about this place,' Fin says, 'Or at least, I've told you what it's helped me to think. If you still feel unsatisfied by the gaps and the dissonances, maybe that's the point. Maybe there are three lessons in *Never Was*.'

'Three lessons? Why does there always have to be three of everything?'

'I think,' says Fin, quickly continuing, 'that for whatever reason, being here impels you to tell your story to somebody, to whoever's here in *Never Was* before you. I told mine to Miss Universe. You've told yours to me, or you've tried to. But just like I have done while sat here on this cliff-edge waiting for that cruise ship to come back to life, you also have to listen to somebody else's story, and you also have to be OK with not knowing the *full* story. Soon you yourself will be in my position, and whoever it is that turns up in your version of *Never Was* and ends up telling their story to you, well, they too will have to make do without knowing your story – not all of it.'

'But you fell asleep through part of mine,' Daniel protests, still stubborn, still resistant. 'You didn't listen to everything. And a minute ago you were saying that knowing without knowing is a kind of privilege.'

'That's true,' says Fin.

'*What* is?' says Daniel.

The sea simmers. The funnel of the cruise ship whistles again. She seems happy, relieved, excited.

'Perhaps the third lesson has to do with being able to speak without being listened to,' Fin says. 'When I fell asleep – why did you carry on talking? Who were you talking to?'

To this, Daniel says nothing.

'Anyway, I have to go,' Fin says, still standing. 'Hug me goodbye?'

'No,' Daniel says, sulkily. *Why would I hug somebody I hardly know?* thinks Daniel, grumpy, nervous, exhausted.

Fin hovers nonetheless. 'Something else did occur to me.'

'What?' asks Daniel, still in the same sulky voice.

'When you spoke about Crystal earlier, about her visit and your breakfast trips to McDonald's, you seemed to think – you seemed to imply – that she sometimes knew exactly what you were thinking. That she sometimes knew what was going on inside you. That she might actually have been psychic.'

Daniel nods curtly.

'Well, that's not supposed to happen out there, is it? *Here* – don't ask me how or why – it's as if you can feel other people's feelings, enter into them, even mix them up a little, like you found yourself doing with Mika's. But outside – out there, wherever *there* is, if it still exists, if *we* do – that's a kind of magic. That's called telepathy and that's called messing with people. Messing with their heads, I mean.'

Daniel blinks blankly.

Fin waits a bit.

'It's almost as if some of *Never Was* went with Crystal when she left.'

'Oh, but she thinks it's the other way round,' Daniel says. 'She thinks she's stuck *here*, or that some of her is. Or that too much of her is. I don't know – I still don't really know what to believe. *Out there*, as you call it, I haven't seen or spoken to Crystal in years. I don't even know where she lives anymore, what country, what continent. But when I heard her voice in the toilet cubicle earlier – if I wasn't just hearing things and it really was Crystal – she implied that this place was her proof to me. That *this* was what she had meant when she said she could prove to me she was a murderer. If that's true – if everything is – her version of *Never Was* must have been terrible. It must have been unbearable! It's hard to understand why being in her version of *Never Was* would have made her sensitive to other people's feelings – why she would have cared at all.'

Fin takes a very deep breath.

The blood stains on Daniel's T-shirt have re-arranged – now six thin red lines sketch the shape of a coffin, just about visible.

'I don't know,' Fin says, staring at the emerging shape. 'I don't know what to say anymore, Daniel.'

Daniel looks up at Fin abruptly. Nobody has ever called Daniel *Daniel* out loud before – *or nobody*, thinks Daniel, *except Crystal just now, if it really was Crystal who found me crying in that toilet cubicle, tears crashing from my eyes, blood thudding from my cold broken nostrils.*

Fin, meanwhile, has turned around. Fin is already walking away from the cliff edge by the time that Daniel...*But that's the wrong direction!*

'Hey! Hey, you're walking the wrong way!' Daniel shouts. 'You live down there – the other way!'

Nothing.

'Hey! Don't leave me alone here! Hey! Please don't go!'

But Fin is already too far away. It's almost dark in *Never Was* now. Fin's slight figure fades into the descending night. Daniel sits back down on the snowy ground, defeated, wearier than ever before.

In the wide rippling sky, a moon appears.

Then another one.

What the fuck?

Snow snows, but the snow is not snow – it's scattered ashes. It's blossom. It's nothing.

The lights of the cruise ship have flickered on. The boat, Daniel notices, is now abuzz – full of life and tinkling with voices. Some kind of party seems to be happening inside her ballrooms. Fin's pterosaur – *or whatever it is*, Daniel thinks – has lifted off again from the helipad. The creature stays close to the ship as she parts the sea's waves, which tease the ship's sides, which glide through the sea slowly but purposively. From Daniel's perspective the ship is gradually lessening in size. *Soon it will be nothing but a dot on the horizon*, Daniel thinks. Fin's pterosaur, too, is quickly diminishing. Soon its body will be but the size of a fly again – soon its body will be nothing but a thin vertical line, briefly balanced above a tiny dot

!

GAME OVER

Exegesis; or, Finasteride

'In the culture represented by the heroes of the Iliad, *the distinction between art and nature, between the artificial and the natural, is not the same as in our modern cultures. Their culture was a song culture [...]. In our modern cultures, artificial implies 'unreal' while natural implies 'real.' In a song culture, by contrast, the artificial can be just as real as the natural, since the words of an 'artificial' song can be just as real as the words of 'natural' speech in a real-life experience. In a song culture, the song can be just as real as life itself.'*

Gregory Nagy, *The Ancient Greek Hero in 24 Hours*

'I want your heart to beat like the wing of a pterosaur.'

Fin, *Jurassic*

'Hi.

Hi?

I'm Fin.

That's F, I, N – no second 'n'. Sometimes I say the second 'n' is unseen and unheard, like a little girl. Nobody laughs at that now though. Nobody remembers the saying – *little girls should be* seen *but not heard* – so they can't correct me. They just look baffled and confused.

Huh. Excuse me while I figure out how to use this old thing.

Hhhhm.

No, I do not want video. Too many wrinkles!

Hhhhm. Huh.

OK, here we go.

I found out about this project a long time ago, possibly before it even existed. A friend told me about it. Their name was Daniel and I met them somewhere called *Never Was*. How can I explain what *Never Was* is? It's difficult. But I've given it some thought and if you like you can imagine it like this – as a video game that has become unplayable, or a sim only playable on obsolescent consoles, on machinery that no longer exists.

Let me be clear. *Never Was* is not a game, but I'm going to explain it to you as if it were.

OK?

OK.

'Daniel', by the way, wasn't necessarily Daniel's real name. Let's say that 'Daniel' was Daniel's 'handle' or the name of their avatar, because *Never Was* is a sim you can enter with your real name or you can invent one, or the programme can generate a name on your behalf. It's up to you, but it makes a difference which option you choose. Everything in *Never Was* has a consequence, though never an obvious one. I played as 'Fin' but I wasn't called Fin when I played, though afterwards, after I left *Never Was*, I became Fin – I changed my IRL name, I mean. *Never Was* can have that kind of effect on you.

Sim is short for *simulation*, in case you're listening to this and you don't know – in case somebody at some point figures out how to listen back to my undulating voice on this ancient contraption. Testosterone eventually lowered my voice, broke it once and for all, but the pitch still clambers back up to its old territory every now and then.

During the time that we were in *Never Was* together, Daniel spoke of some salt mines in 'the North' being transformed into archives after years of disarray and disuse, but I didn't know then what 'the North' signified, where it was, what country, what continent. I sometimes felt as if Daniel might have entered *Never Was* from a different point in time than me, even from a different version of the world. They often spoke of people and things I'd never heard of, or that my avatar had never heard of, or that the part of me that my avatar was a manifestation of had never heard of. It's complicated. In other ways Daniel seemed so much younger than me – not immature necessarily, just oddly unaware.

Hhhhm.

When I say the word *world*, I mean something different to *globe* or *planet*. *World* is a word for trust and predictability, the luxury of consistency, and simultaneously the illusion of it. The world is the way I can take my eyes off the horizon knowing that the sun will still rise. Some people have never been there, the world.

Hhhmm.

This isn't coming out quite as I intended.

OK.

The thing is, *Never Was* reads you. When you first enter, the landscape mostly belongs to your *listener*, the person who was there in *Never Was* before you and who then befriends you. You're suspended in this upended mesh of places and times that's some kind of materialisation of your *listener*'s lost dreams and disappointments, a landscape assembled from things your *listener* has longed for or just briefly wanted, missed opportunities they didn't even realise they'd missed.

And sometimes, as happened with me, your character or avatar in *Never Was* is similarly assembled from aspects of yourself that have fallen by the wayside – elements of yourself that never came to be.

But for a while the version of *Never Was* you enter isn't yours. It isn't to do with you – you aren't the protagonist. Then gradually you are. Gradually you find yourself recognising things. I think the pairings make the transition possible – I think you're paired with people whose version of *Never Was* shares something with yours. It's not necessarily obvious what though. With Daniel, I felt like we had a lot in common. We were both sad in a bratty way, out of our bodies and unlikely scholars, and we were both weathered addicts. We were similar in many ways, Daniel and I. Almost interchangeable, I'd go so far as to say, and in a way the game seemed to depend on that interchangeability, on the possibility of proximity of experience. But on the other hand, my own *listener* was different to me. She was comfortable with the contours of her body, proud of having once been otherwise, and in *Never Was* she was known as Miss Universe. Unlike Daniel and me, she wasn't white.

I was still confused by the time Daniel arrived, but I was different already. Something had shifted already. It's hard to describe.

Hhhm. OK.

I think a lot of trans folk play *Never Was*, by the way, or else people turn out to be trans having played, but you don't necessarily have to be trans to play.

In his account of ancient Greek song culture, Nagy says that recollection *is* the 'reliving of an experience'. 'If you "recall" someone else's experience by way of song or music,' he says, 'then that experience and all its emotions become your own, even if they had not been originally yours.'

Hhhm.

I'm slowly coming round to what I intended to say. Bear with me. I'm old. Jurassic. Ancient.

Another crucial aspect of *Never Was* is the narrative level, which is also your *listener*'s leaving level, the way the sim comes to an end for them. As the *storyteller* you tell three stories about your life, which is how the game finishes 'reading' your character or avatar, how it finishes assembling your version of *Never Was*. The scene of your speaking is also significant. You're still in your *listener*'s version when you begin, but by the time you finish, the scenery has shifted. In the meantime your *listener* listens, and by listening, learns how to leave.

Sometimes as a *listener* it felt like you could intervene, like you could nudge the *storyteller*'s narrative by interpreting it.

I don't know how important that was.

I don't know how exactly *Never Was* allows you inside other people's minds either – how you have access there to other people's interiority, or feel like you have. Like Daniel did Mika's. I don't know if that's innate to *Never Was* or whether it's something that has accumulated over time on account of *Never Was* having been moved through by multiple people, something learned or learning, like an algorithm.

For the Greeks – I said this to Daniel too – *kleos* meant both fame and the song that made the fame known, the manner in which somebody's life came to be heard. As a kid, for reasons I won't go into, I believed I was famous and I behaved that way, kept waiting and waiting for somebody, anybody, to recognise me. As I got older, the fantasy escaped me. Then I went to *Never Was*, entered my fantasy's future memoir, left, and instead of waiting to be heard without saying a word, I said something.

I'm not a little girl and I'm not a woman, I said. Never was. Ha!

But in any case, what I meant to say, what I wanted to record for this project, this archive, was – how can I put it?

Hhhhm.

I felt compelled to invent an alternative ending for my and Daniel's encounter. *Alternative ending* isn't quite the right phrase. It's written from the perspective of *Never Was* itself, though obviously that's an impossible perspective. I should also note that I don't know how Daniel left, because I wasn't there. I never saw Daniel's version of *Never Was* – not completely. As I imagined the ending from *Never Was*'s perspective, the two characters sitting on the cliffside are always the *same* characters, just played by different people – the same characters, differently inhabited. It's like a composite of all the endings that have ever taken place in *Never Was*.

Don't laugh.

Or do.

Who cares if anybody's even listening. I'm old. Going, going, almost gone. Did you know that *Finasteride*, my almost-namesake, is a drug they give to men to counteract receding hairlines? I've taken it myself, but it didn't work.

OK. Enough.

Here goes.

Hhhhm.

The deckchairs were waiting for them when they reached the clifftop, as they always had been, as it seemed they ever would be. Above them in the swirly sky, two crescent moons now jostled, their cusps just touching, their colour pinky orange. In the distance on the rim of a swirl skimmed a single gull – unless the gull was a pterosaur. About that the pair often argued. About that the two of them could never agree.

The one leant down to a mound of snow that stood heaped between the deckchairs, and pulled out two cans of Pepsi.

Thanks, said the other.

This was what they'd done every time, ever since their first meeting – sit on the cliffside side by side. They had both been through many changes in the meantime, many experiences, many genders, and both were always a little anxious, in their respective fashions, about what exactly it meant for them to be here, in *Never Was*. Each was always nervous of the other too, at first, but soon enough distrust would dissipate. They drank their Pepsis and settled down to wait for the sunset. Eventually they came to understand that it was not the sunset they were waiting for, but something else, something at once simpler and more complicated.

Before their eyes a cruise ship, once wrecked, hauled itself back from its bedridden state, belched, and headed off – salt crusting its recovered sides – to its next destination.

'I'm always a bit sorry to see it go,' said one of them.

'Yes,' the other answered. 'Me too, though cruise ships are terrible.'

Hhhm.

For a while they watched the bob and plop of polymer ornaments upon the sea's frothy surface, and then they parted, melancholic but content. It was a difficult thing to describe, the sight, the encounter. It always seemed to them both as if they had shared something.

When eventually the pair returned – as they had done and would do, over and over – the cruise ship was there again, returned to its sorry state. They sat in the deckchairs and chatted a little, told stories. Their heels, in recent years, were tickled by grains of tobacco sand: at some point somebody had dumped tons of the stuff on the beach below in an attempt to halt the coast's erosion, and miraculously the trick had worked, and both of them had had to come to terms with the world's return – with the unlikely lovely grim of it.

That was what the cruiser was all about, too, they'd come to understand, eventually. That was what they were here for, what they came back to do every time—

To watch the world come and go

and not to be too wrecked by it.'

fin

Miss Universe's Last Word

'For the sake of a name, let's call it Nonetown.'

The woman speaking places her Pepsi back on its foamy mat. She's sat at the bar's bar, heels clinking a high stool. Her blouse is satin, a light shade of purple. Her earrings, dangling things that tickle the soft hairs of her neck, have amber, not turquoise, stones in them.

'Let me explain.'

The body she's speaking to shuffles a bit. The bar's hot with bodies, bursting. The bumpy air has a brackish tang to it, the taste of condensed sweatiness. It's late – a stretch past midnight. Some of the bodies have come on from Finnochio's, some have been here all evening, some, when this place closes, will cross over the road to Compton's, the evergreen eternally-open cafeteria where the tender queers tend to gather. There's no McDonald's in this strip of town – not yet – and no queen would be seen dead in McDonald's anyway.

'OK honey?'

She's a queen, sure, but she's also Miss Universe. Or she was once, in *Never Was.*

The body she's talking to mumbles something, wafts a cartwheeling fly away. The body belongs to somebody who looks not unlike Daniel, your erstwhile so-called protagonist. They're scrawny, white, somewhere between boyish and soft butch, handsome, but not Daniel. They're not Fin either. Neither Fin nor Daniel live here, in this time and place. But where they are, they're about to be grateful for it.

Miss Universe taps her emptied Pepsi with a long

manicured nail, signals subtly to the barman for another. She's sober these days, mostly. Every so often she dips her finger for a dab when its offered, but she doesn't get cravings, doesn't feel like she's really needed it since—

—But wait, hang on a minute.

We don't know what Miss Universe is thinking.

But we can see her, and we can hear her.

She's takes a slow luscious sip on her fresh Pepsi. The body beside her knocks back a beer. Three emptied bottles already sit on the counter, their plucked lids strewn among them.

'Let's say that Nonetown is the name of the place that *Never Was* makes in *this* world. OK?'

The boy-cum-soft-butch beside Miss Universe nods quickly, eyes scanning the bar and its jostling bodies. Whoever they are they seem jumpy, not uncomfortable necessarily, but nervy. Their forrid and back are contributing strongly to the room's dense layers of sweatiness. Maybe it's the first time they've been in this kind of bar – maybe they're a young homophile, a nascent lesbo, a newbie in the neon city. It's the mid-sixties, after all, and though this strip of town in San Francisco belongs to the queers, this kid isn't from San Francisco. This kid is—

—But wait, what? It's the mid-sixties? In San Francisco?

In a second or so Miss Universe is about to explain how, though she's sitting in a bar in SF in the mid-sixties before George Michael or Princess Di or the Internet, she knows about *Never Was*. But first she lifts her handbag up to her hugged knees, takes out a clam-shell-shaped mirror, checks her lipstick, untangles two eyelashes. Across the room the bell of the bar door makes itself heard above into the music and chatter. Miss Universe arches a tidy eyebrow as two more queens make an entrance, with them three faggots, all of them white, like the body sat next to her.

'This place never used to be so *pale*,' Miss Universe sighs.

Then she swallows. When she speaks again, it's in a different register.

'What you have to remember, honey, is that there are as many *expressions* of Never Was as there are *versions*. OK?'

The boy-cum-soft-butch beside her says nothing. Miss Universe elbows the cage of the kid's skinny ribs. '*OK?*'

'OK.'

'OK then.'

And then in her own words Miss Universe goes on to say that while each *version* depends on the person, on their peculiar desires and lingering losses, each *expression* of *Never Was* is basically a *portal* – a way in, an entry. Anything will do, so long as it's capable of giving *Never Was* form. It could be a daydream, it could be a movie, it could be, *oh*, who knows, a song, a drag ball, and once upon a time it might have been a—

—But let's just hear it as Miss Universe says it, shall we?

'Nobody ever enters the same way simultaneously. No two people go through the same portal at the same time. Whoever you end up meeting in *Never Was* could have come in from anywhere and anywhen, though whomever you end up befriending there also depends on a number of factors, unexpected affinities, cute correspondences. Now, you might be inclined to imagine that in *my* case the portal was something like a nightclub, somewhere like Finnochio's, which, honey, if you've never yet been, is where us so-called "female impersonators" sing for our supper as opposed to working the street—'

She pauses, scans the body of the boy-cum-softbutch beside her—

'You, my dear, will have your troubles, but you'll find a nice job eventually. You'll do OK. My options, however, are skinnier than your ribs. For the time being.'

She sips on her Pepsi, inspects the fake moons in her painted nails.

'But as I was saying, my portal, my expression of *Never Was*, was not, as I imagine you might have presumptively imagined, a nightclub. I'm not telling you *what* it was though – oh no! My *version* of *Never Was*, on the other hand, now that would need a whole *novel* to tell you about.'

She laughs, scowls, laughs again. She lives at El Rosa's Hotel round the corner, rents a room there. The key's buried, right now, between her breasts, deep down between them.

'I, my newbie friend, was the winner of the beauty pageant for all time. Held in Miami, would you believe.'

The group that entered the bar a few moments ago have now made their way to the space at the counter opposite. One of them wafts the same fly that earlier was wafted by the quiet kid Miss Universe's currently speaking to. The fly bounces in the bumpy air, comes down hungrily on a spilt splash of liquor.

'Anyway, just as there are many expressions of *Never Was*, so too are there many ways of leaving. But whatever way you leave, you always take some of *Never Was* with you, OK? Not *too* much, mind, but something. Well now, Nonetown is the collective noun for all of those little somethings. I *said* it was a place, but it's more like – *hhmm*, a change. It's my name for the change made by in this world by *Never Was*. Following?'

The body beside her looks back at her blankly, smiles clumsily, pushes a button on their shirt in and out, out and in, of its buttonhole. The button is the colour of turquoise, not amber.

'Jeeez, honey.'

The fly slurps the last of its puddle of liquor, happily collapses.

'OK. You see that dashing young homophile stood over there? The one with the highly commendable bone structure? He comes from a town in sunny Pennsylvania, a coal-mining town as a matter of fact. A couple years back some workers set fire to a trash pile in the town's cemetery, and the flames made their way down into the old mines. Nothing happened at first. Then cracks in the ground appeared and out of them dashed great clouds of smoke. Imagine! The smoke was poison. Toxic. Carbon monoxide. But that's by the by. I *know* that that darling young man's been to *Never Was* because of something on his neck that looks like a birthmark but isn't quite, and I know he carries some of Nonetown around with him because—*well.*'

'He has a sad kind of look in his eye.' It's the first full sentence the boy-cum-soft-butch has said since we've been here, listening.

Miss Universe grins. The red velvet walls of the bar are all covered with framed photographs. Miss Universe herself is beaming from one of them. She's stood on a beach, her back to the sea, her costume the same light shade of purple of the blouse she's now wearing. Some of other frames are empty and one of the empty frames hangs, skewwhiff, behind the profile of the kid Miss Universe is speaking to.

'Oh that's just because he knows the sorry fate of his hometown. He knows a little bit about how it feels to live up close to the waste and detritus of the New World. And he knows he's queer.'

The boy-cum-soft-butch flinches at this, quickly asks the barman for another bottle of beer. The barman hesitates. Miss Universe tilts her head. Just like that, the beer appears.

The kid drinks. They seem like they're about to ask Miss Universe a question, but Miss Universe interrupts them before they begin.

'Don't even think about asking me where *I* come from, honey.'

The kid-cum-boy-cum-soft-butch-body stares down at their own scrawny thighflesh. Miss Universe sighs, swivels around on her stool, taps the shoulder of somebody standing behind her. When she swivels back, a lit *Lucky* hangs nimbly from her lips. Smoke swirls from the corner of her mouth.

'The last person to ask me *that* was that bitch Crystal.'

'Who?'

'Never mind. Listen, kidda – can I call you kidda? *Honey* is running dry on my tongue.'

'Sure.'

'Now, I can tell you're not stupid. I know you know how this so-called New World was made by taking land and making people *into* property, *hhhhm*?? Gold, silver, petroleum, bodies. It's all about extraction. Ordinariness is never *not* a kind of cipher for catastrophe – just think of the English, sipping their tea. Oil was *supposed* to take over from slavery and if you ask me all this fuss and bother of being one or the other – of being a man or a woman, I mean – is just another tiresome byproduct of capitalism. They need to know who they're exploiting, kidda, in order to do so effectively. But anyway, soon enough, not too far in the future, the weather created by all this craziness is gonna come take its revenge. It's just that some of us feel the weather ahead of its coming.'

She pauses.

'Look, I get it. Whatever it is, it's enough to send you wild with sorrow, huh kidda? Well, Nonetown is a name for *seeing* the sorrow, instead of being it.'

She puffs on her *Lucky*.

Swallows the last of her Pepsi.

Woozy, the body beside her listens intently. The kid-cum-boy-cum-soft-butch-body has been listening intently ever since they arrived here, stepped tentatively over the threshold, made their way over to this side of the bar, climbed onto a high stool, and found themselves sat next to Miss Universe. The kid will still be listening when, later this evening or early morning, when the lightbulbs in the bar become the rising sun splashing through glazed blurry windowpanes, Miss Universe bundles them over to Compton's, café to queens and transsexuals and faggots and a dyke or two too, orders coffees, gossips, gazes into her clam-shell-shaped mirror, chats on to the boy-cum-soft-butch-whatever and then, when a cop comes in and attempts to remove her without rhyme or reason, chucks her coffee in his pink crinkled face, and starts a riot.

Sometimes people in glass houses have to throw stones.

Same goes for plastic snowglobes.

Locations, In Order of Appearance

The Afterparty (the Sand Dunes, the Ha Ha,
Fin's Mansion, the Cliff Edge)

The North (McDonald's, the Salt Mine,
the Great Subsidence)

The Club (the Toilet Cubicle, the K-hole)

The Archive (The Salt Mine)

SF

Acknowledgements

For a long time, *Never Was* felt more like a puzzle or conundrum I couldn't solve – but *had* to – than a work of fiction. As it turned out, the puzzle itself pulled me through, but I wouldn't ever have finished it were it not for friends and lovers who should hopefully already know who they are, if they've read this far. My thanks and gratitude, too, to Jack and Ellis at Cipher for seeing what I was trying to do in *Never Was* better, I think, than I could.